MAPP'S RETURN

Mapp's Return – A story of Mapp & Lucia in the Style of the Originals by E.F.Benson
Hugh Ashton

ISBN-13: 978-1-912605-69-9

ISBN-10: 1-91-260569-4

Published by j-views Publishing, 2020

© 2020 Hugh Ashton & j-views Publishing

All rights reserved. Without limiting the rights under copyright reserved above, no part of this publication may be reproduced, stored in or introduced into a retrieval system, or transmitted, in any form, or by any means (electronic, mechanical, photocopying, recording, or otherwise) without the prior written permission of both the copyright owner and the above publisher of this book.

This is a work of fiction. Names, characters, places, brands, media, and incidents are either the product of the author's imagination or are written in respectful tribute to the creator of the principal characters.

www.HughAshtonBooks.com

www.j-views.biz

publish@j-views.biz

j-views Publishing, 26 Lombard Street, Lichfield, WS13 6DR, UK

Contents

Introduction IV
One 1
Two 8
Three 13
Four 22
Five 26
Six 35
Seven 45
Eight 49
Nine 56
Ten 63
Eleven 73
Twelve 79
Thirteen 85
Fourteen 91
Fifteen 97
Sixteen 104
Seventeen 110
Eighteen 117
Nineteen 125
Twenty 131
Twenty-one 136
Twenty-two 140
If you enjoyed this story.... 149
About the Author 151

INTRODUCTION

This is my second Mapp and Lucia pastiche, and I have to say that in many ways it came much easier than *Mapp at Fifty*. I had learned more about the characters, and about the language, and I found myself slipping happily into the little paradoxes and contradictions that form such a delightful part of life in Tilling.

Even so, I discovered new aspects to the characters, or rather, aspects that somehow get overlooked. Georgie, for example, is much more than the clothes-horse that he might at first appear to be, and Lucia, vain and frivolous as she might be at times, undeniably has her more serious side. We've never seen the stepfather side of Algergon Wyse. He strikes me, though, as the sort of man who would take his responsibilities to Isabel Poppit seriously, and I've tried to bring that out.

I've been trying to work out my favourite character as I have been writing this. I think we are all fond of Georgie, and we have some sort of admiration for Lucia. But when we look at the cast of characters objectively, the only Tillingite who has really achieved anything substantial is Irene Coles, with her Picture of the Year at the Royal Academy. The quaint one became quite real to me as the story developed, and it was fun to give her a key role in the plot, rather than just a walk-on part.

As far as the actual writing is concerned, there are ironies galore scattered throughout the originals, and these are a joy to drop into the story. Benson's characters rarely say what is on their mind, and it is necessary to alert the reader, who might otherwise take their words at face value. I may not be Oscar Wilde, let alone Fred Benson, but I do enjoy my little attempts at *bons mots*.

Special thanks are once again due to the Mapp and Lucia group on Facebook who have encouraged me to hope that this little offering will not be completely unpleasing to you. I am hoping that this, my second story, will not be

INTRODUCTION

my last such visit to Tilling, as there is so much more to write about. So, dear ones, once more I will not bid you farewell at this time, but *Au reservoir*.

Hugh Ashton, Lichfield, 2020

MAPP'S RETURN

A STORY OF MAPP & LUCIA IN THE STYLE OF THE ORIGINALS BY E.F.BENSON

HUGH ASHTON

J-VIEWS PUBLISHING, LICHFIELD, UK

One

Autumn was approaching, and the wind swept over the Sussex marshes, accompanied by blasts of chilling rain which rattled against the windowpanes at Grebe, home of Major Benjamin and Mrs Elizabeth Mapp-Flint.

"Don't use too much," she warned her husband, who had risen from his armchair to feed the dismal fire with more coal, and to prod it into some semblance of life. "I read that there may be another of those coal-strikes this winter and the price may go up to double what it is now. If there is any coal at all to be had, that is."

One

"Well, it's pretty cold in this room," the Major. "I don't seem to have been properly warm for a week." He shivered.

"Then perhaps you'd like us to move into one of those little cottages that Lucia made us all pay for when she was Mayor – the horrid red-brick ones that the council built along the Hastings road." She also shivered, but whether it was in disgust at the red-brickness of the houses, Lucia's perfidy in daring to suggest something which she (Elizabeth) would have suggested herself had she been in a position to do so, or simply from cold (for the room was indeed somewhat chilly), it was impossible to say.

"Of course not," he answered her, though if truth be told, a workman's hovel currently seemed more congenial than Grebe at this time – provided, that is, that the Major occupied it in solitary splendour, and was not sharing it with his wife, who had been in a foul temper ever since her disastrous birthday party some months previously.

"Of course not," he repeated, and retreated to the depths of his armchair. It was clear though, even to the Major's usually unperceptive eye, that something more than usual was amiss.

"Anything the matter, Liz?" he asked, gruffly, but not unaffectionately.

"We must be seen again," she answered. The truth was, that since her birthday party, Elizabeth had adopted Lord Salisbury's policy of 'splendid isolation'. Not only had she ceased to issue invitations to bridge-parties, tea-parties and the like, but any invitations (and these were few enough) that happened to drop through the letterbox to such social events went, after a brief reading and a sniff of dismissal, into the kitchen fireplace.

If Elizabeth had been asked on what principle she was acting, she would have been hard pushed to give a reasonable answer, but the truth of the matter was that she feared the mockery of Tilling society after the events of her fiftieth birthday party. In her own eyes, she was disgraced for ever in the eyes of those whom she had previously regarded as her equals in social rank, and this disgrace had sprung from the actions of her own husband.

There was, however, the pleasure in knowing that her and Major Benjy's (for such was the name she had bestowed on him, even before their marriage, when he was simply Major Flint, and she a mere Miss Elizabeth Mapp) absence from the social events of Tilling would present difficulties in the making up of foursomes for bridge, and other social occasions.

Even so, the continued isolation was starting to grate on her. Major Benjy's powers of conversational invention, never the strongest point of his character, revolved chiefly around himself. There were limits to how many times she was prepared to listen with equanimity to an account of some savage Indian wild beast laying down its life as the result of the Major's actions, or to how he had made a hole in two when playing golf against the late Captain Puffin with the aid of a spoon cleek or a mashie putter, or some such strangely-named implement.

She desired – nay, hungered for – conversation on matters of more importance. For example, had Diva introduced any new items into her tea-time menus, and, more importantly, had she somehow managed to serve them without burning or otherwise spoiling them? Had the Padre and Evie been to Ireland again for their holiday, and if so, was his speech now replete with 'begorra's and 'to be sure's? And, most important of all, what hideous schemes were now being hatched in Mallards, as it had been known in Mappian days, but now rechristened Mallards House (but never referred to as such by her), where Lucia and Georgie Pillson now resided?

There might be something noble in the concept of Achilles sulking in his tent, but Elizabeth, for one, found this particular instance of nobility to be somewhat overrated, and she was willing to believe that her spouse found it to be even more so.

"Benjy, dear," she called over to the armchair. "It occurs to me that Withers has been doing the marketing for some time now. Maybe you could take over those duties tomorrow, since the weather promises to be a little better. There are one or two little items where your knowledge and experience would be more useful than those of Withers, worthy as she is."

"Will you be coming with me?" asked the Major.

"No. As I mentioned to you at breakfast, my ankle is a little sore, and I do not trust myself to walk into Tilling and back, particularly in this weather."

Major Benjy scratched his head in a vain attempt to remember what had been said at breakfast. Try as he might, he could remember nothing of a conversation regarding his wife's health. This was hardly surprising, for

ONE

this conversation had taken place only in Elizabeth's head some minutes before.

"Oh, very well," he said in an attempt to sound resigned. In truth, he was as bored with this policy of social ostracism (that is to say, Tilling society being ostracised by the Mapp-Flints) as his wife. He considered to himself that there was a chance of running into some acquaintance who would stand him a drink.

The recent spell of bad weather had prevented him from playing golf, even if there had been an opponent whom he considered worthy of a match, and in any case, Elizabeth had taken to searching his pockets (on the pretext of checking for a clean handkerchief) before he set out for his game, and removing any money or objects that she deemed in excess of what was required for transport out to the links. Accordingly Benjy was deprived of his formerly customary post-match tipple from a hip-flask, or even from the clubhouse bar, and he felt the lack most keenly.

Needless to say, since the night of the birthday party, intoxicating drink of any kind was no longer to be found in the Mapp-Flint household, and the Major was forced to listen to his wife's tirades without the comforting anaesthetic of a whisky and soda. The prospect of a respite from this enforced Saharan abstinence played powerfully upon his imagination.

"I will need a list," he told Elizabeth.

"Of course you will," she smiled at him. If truth be told, she was scarcely less happy than him at the prospect of release from their self-proclaimed lazaretto. With luck, Major Benjy would fall into conversation with at least one person who would help to reduce the level of ignorance at Grebe regarding the other inhabitants of Tilling.

Nor (for she knew her husband better than he realised) would she be unduly concerned if the acquisition of this precious knowledge involved the imbibing of intoxicating liquors. This would be a small price to pay for the information that she was sure he would be able to bring back and pour inter her greedy ears.

Satisfied, she reached forward and placed another lump of coal (albeit a small one) on the fire.

Two

In Mallards House, Lucia Pillson and Georgie were sitting companionably in front of a roaring fire.

Lucia was engaged in a study of Dante's *Paradiso*, with the aid of a thick Italian-English dictionary and an English translation. It was at least the third time she had undertaken this quest, and she was beginning to feel that the game might not, after all, be worth the candle.

Increasingly, the Italian text and the dictionary were consulted less and less, and more time was spent with the English.

"Listen, Georgie, is this not beautiful?" she asked him. "'*L'amor che move: i sole e l'altre stelle*'," she declaimed in those veiled tones which had been used to such effect in so many dramatic performances.

"It sounds nice," said Georgie. He was busily engaged in embroidering some cushion covers for the easy chair in his upstairs sitting-room. The floral pattern was a copy of a detail in a Gobelin tapestry hanging in Versailles, and he had taken pains to procure silks of the precise shades needed to reproduce the original. "What does it mean?"

Happily, Lucia hardly needed the "crib" to provide him with an answer. "Why," she said, "it is love which moves the sun and the stars."

Georgie frowned. "But it is not the sun and the stars which move," he pointed out. "At least they didn't when I was at school. It is we who move and the sun stands still, and the moon also moves around us. And the stars stand still – I think." He turned again to his petit point.

Lucia appeared to consider this. "Perhaps it was different in Dante's day," she said at length. "In fact, I am sure it was. All kinds of things are different now."

Georgie was unconvinced on the matter, but held his peace. "What is happening at Grebe, do you think?" he asked Lucia, in an attempt to change the subject. "Now that is something that is different. Before— well, you know, before

Two

the birthday party, Elizabeth was in town every day, ears open for the latest news. And Major Benjy was to be seen as well, but I haven't seen either of them in town for weeks, maybe months now. Or bridge, or tea at Diva's, or our little evening parties. Have you been sending out invitations to them for our parties?"

"I have, and I have received no reply." Lucia said.

"Are they both sick? Or are they even still living at Grebe?" Georgie asked.

"According to Grosvenor, who meets Withers from time to time, they would appear to be both healthy, and living at Grebe, if the groceries and produce she is ordering are any kind of guide."

"So they've shut themselves away? What have we done?"

"I suppose," Lucia said reflectively, "that some might claim that we stole Elizabeth's sister from her when she moved in here from Grebe."

"But you and I know that is not so," said Georgie. "And in any case, the Wyses and the Padre and Diva had nothing to do with any of that, and they are being ignored, too." He embroidered another petal, put down his needle, and sighed. "You know, I never thought I would ever say this, but I miss Elizabeth in much the same way that you miss spices in food. They may cause a little discomfort at times, but they do make life much more interesting than if they are not present."

Lucia laughed. "Just fancy! Comparing Elizabeth to a spice! But yes, you are right. However, Figgis delivered a message to me from Mr Wyse this afternoon, asking if he might be permitted to call on me tomorrow morning."

"This sounds as though it might be interesting," said Georgie. "Do you know what he wants to see you about?"

"He simply referred to a rather delicate personal matter."

"Oh dear. I hope that Susan has not become – what was his term again – 'unhinged'? again as she so nearly did when her Blue Birdie passed away."

"So do I. But I do not think that is the reason for this. I saw Susan just this morning as I was marketing. She was ordering some rather extravagant out-of-season strawberries from Twistevant's, and she seemed perfectly in command of herself when she and I exchanged a few pleasant words."

"Something to do with the Contessa, perhaps?"

Two

"It is certainly possible, I suppose. Oh dear." Lucia stopped suddenly.

"What is it?"

"If you are right, and this delicate matter is connected to the Contessa, maybe he will need me to translate some Italian letters or some such."

"That should be no problem, surely? You have a dictionary – with that you can make sense of any letter."

"But if he presents me with the letter and asks for an immediate translation?"

"Tarsome," Georgie admitted. "But perhaps it is nothing to do with the Contessa."

"Oh, I do hope you are right, Georgie. Perhaps you could be with me when he comes to call? Your support would be most welcome."

"Certainly, if Mr Wyse permits it."

Three

Mr Wyse called on Lucia precisely at the arranged time of eleven o'clock the next morning.

"It is most generous of you to give your time to my – or perhaps I should say our – little problem," he began.

"I will certainly attempt to be of assistance. May my husband join us? I believe I heard him come in just now. As two heads are said to be better than one, maybe three will be better than two?"

"Certainly, certainly," Mr Wyse told her.

Georgie had just returned from marketing, having arranged matters so that he arrived immediately after having seen Mr Wyse enter the house. He was clearly in a state of some agitation, but after being admitted to the garden-room to join Lucia and Algernon Wyse, he caontained his excitement admirably.

Mr Wyse appeared to be more than a little embarrassed as he began his explanation. "My dear Mrs Pillson, and Mr Pillson." He bowed slightly to each as he addressed them by name. "I am deeply grateful for the kindness you are doing me here this morning by agreeing to listen to my account of our little problem. I say that it is 'our problem' because although it affects me, it touches Susan more closely. It is a most personal and distressing matter, and we are anxious to keep the details, and indeed, the very existence of the problem itself, as closely guarded as possible. I trust that you understand this very delicate state of affairs."

"Naturally," Lucia and Georgie answered him, almost in unison.

"You are aware," Mr Wyse continued, "that Susan has a daughter by her previous marriage, Isabel by name?"

"Indeed so," Georgie answered him. "It is she from whom I purchased a lease of Mallards Cottage before I— I moved to this house."

"Of course. I confess that I had almost forgotten that fact," admitted Mr Wyse. "Isabel, though a charming young lady—"

"Delightful," interjected Lucia, whose last memory of Isabel Poppit was of an unkempt, sun-browned Valkyrie bestriding a noisy, foul-smelling motorcycle.

Mr Wise bowed at the compliment. "Yes, indeed. Charming and delightful as she is, Isabel has always exhibited a somewhat independent streak in her character, if I may be permitted to use the expression."

Lucia, well aware that the 'independent streak' referred to by Mr Wyse included living in a meanly-furnished fisherman's hut in the sand-dunes, and spending much of the summer lying outside in an almost indecent state of undress until her skin approached the colour and texture of a kipper, nodded her agreement.

"This summer, my sister Amelia, the Contessa Faraglione invited her to spend a few weeks at Capri with her and Cecco – the Count, you understand."

This time it was Georgie's head which signified understanding.

"Susan and I could see no objection, and indeed, we considered it to be a way of expanding Isabel's intellectual and cultural horizons. We provided her with the money to purchase the tickets, and she duly arrived at Capri, where Amelia and Cecco made her welcome."

Three

He paused in his narrative. "I trust that I have made myself clear so far?"

"Indeed you have," Georgie assured him.

"However, we received a letter from my sister informing us that Isabel had formed a most undesirable attachment to an Italian lad – a young man of apparently slender means – Amelia tells us that he has been earning his living as a fisherman of some kind – and without wishing to appear indelicate, we may well assume that he, in common with so many of his countrymen, will have a past that does not stand up to close scrutiny."

"Most fearsome and distressing," said Georgie.

"You have discovered the *mots justes*, if I may be permitted the phrase," Mr Wyse told him. "Susan was most distressed at the thought of her daughter making such a match."

"This is more than – how shall I put it – a mere summer romance, I take it?" asked Lucia. "You believe that Isabel intends marriage with this Italian boy?"

"From the tone of Amelia's letter, and from a letter from Isabel herself which arrived yesterday, we fear this to be the case. She is of age, and we have no legal power to forbid any ties she may choose to make. However, she has announced her intention to return to Tilling, and to stay with Susan and myself for a few weeks."

"Surely that is some cause for relief?" asked Lucia.

"It is indeed, and we would be happy and, as you say, relieved if that were all. However, she has also announced her intention to bring with her this Italian so that we may meet him." He paused. "I need hardly mention, I am sure, that neither Susan nor I feel any compulsion to offer him our hospitality, and I therefore come to make a request of you. It is a great imposition, and if you refuse my request, neither Susan or I will be in the least offended." He continued, "We feel that if we were to refuse Isabel the opportunity to bring Paolo Alberghi, for that is the boy's name, to Tilling, it would throw her into his arms, so to speak. However, we do not feel able to accept him as a guest under our roof, given the delicate emotional state that seems to exist between Isabel and this fisher lad."

Here Mr Wyse's customary urbanity appeared to desert him, and he paused, almost expectantly, as if waiting for Lucia to finish his sentence on his behalf. However, neither Lucia not Georgie seemed in any hurry to do so, and

Three

Mr Wyse was forced to take up the narrative himself. "To make a long and very presumptuous request as briefly as possible, Susan and I would like to ask you to accept this Italian lad as a paying guest in your home. You may take it for granted that Susan and I will recompense you for whatever you think is appropriate for his board and keep."

There was a long silence, at the end of which Mr Wyse spoke. "I understand," he said. "I apologise for even having raised the matter with you. Pray accept my sincere apologies."

"No, no, by no means," replied Lucia. "Please do not take my hesitation as a refusal. I am merely somewhat taken by surprise."

"Perhaps I should explain Susan's and my thinking with regard to this matter. We have not been told, but I think we may safely assume, that this lad's English will be somewhat less than perfect. If he is to come to Tilling, it would be kindness to lodge him in a place where Italian is understood and spoken. Mallards House would seem the obvious choice, given your and Mr Pillson's," here he bowed to both, "proficiency in the Italian language. My Italian is elementary, to say the least, and I fear Susan has only a few words."

At first, it would appear that Lucia had fallen

into a trap, largely of her own making, based on the perception (which she had done nothing to dispel) that she and Georgie could prattle away in fluent Italian, and indeed did so all the time. This was not the first time that such an assumption had led to a crisis; Lucia still inwardly shuddered at memories of meals with Signor Cortese, the composer, and a dinner with Mr Wyse's sister, Amelia, which had been avoided, largely due to Georgie's ingenuity. However, in this case, so long as she was not called upon to play the part of interpreter between this youth and the Wyses, it might be possible to accommodate this guest. There was also the possibility, she mused, that he would be able to help her achieve a real proficiency in the language. Naturally, she could not expect a mere fisherman to provide her with learned criticism of Dante, but her simple robust Italian (and that of Georgie) could no doubt be improved.

There was also the possibility of being the first to know of developments on the Poppit-Wyse front. This was a point that could not be reasonably ignored or put aside. She turned to Georgie. "What is your opinion? A man's advice in these matters is always welcome."

She knew her husband well enough to be

Three

reasonably certain of his agreement, which came as expected.

"We are all of one mind, then," she smiled. "How pleasant to find ourselves all in harmony! When might we expect our guest?"

"My dear Mrs Pillson, you and your husband are too kind." Mr Wyse appeared to be in the throes of intense embarrassment, and he paused for a considerable time before continuing with his speech. "There is, however, one other request that I would make of you, but I quite understand if you find it impossible to comply with this."

"Yes?"

"I hesitate to suggest this, but while this young man is residing with you, if you could make an attempt to dissuade him from marrying Isabel, Susan and I would be most grateful. I would not dream of imposing this as a condition, you understand, but if there is one person in Tilling whom I believe capable of persuading this youth of the folly and the disastrous consequences of this ill-considered liaison, it is you, Mrs Pillson."

"I understand," said Lucia reflectively. "You flatter me. I suppose I can at least promise to examine the situation when this – Paolo, you said? arrives, and if the ground seems promisingly fertile, to sow the appropriate seeds."

"I feel that I am unable to ask for any more," Mr Wyse told her. "My heartfelt thanks for your understanding and for your assistance in this matter, to which I would like to add those of Susan, who will be greatly relieved when I return with the news. As you imagine, this business has been a great strain on her, and I will be happy to be the bearer of glad tidings, if I may express it in those terms."

"When may we expect the arrival of this young man?" Lucia asked once more.

"Isabel has informed us that she expects to arrive in Tilling with him next Tuesday – that is to say, in five days' time. As to the financial side of the matter, I trust that you will provide me with a full account of any expenses that you may incur with respect to this business and I will recompense you immediately."

"Thank you," Lucia said. "That will be most satisfactory."

Mr Wyse rose, and, bowing again to Lucia and Georgie, let himself out.

Four

"Well," said Georgie, when the front door had closed behind Mr Wyse, who could be seen making his way home down the street. "This *is* going to be exciting!"

Lucia, however, seemed to be unable to share his excitement and appeared to be sunk in thought. "How does one dissuade a young man from an unsuitable marriage? I confess that I have no idea." Her usual light-hearted tone appeared to have deserted her, and she had assumed an air of great seriousness.

"Nor I," Georgie told her, "but I am sure that it depends to a large extent upon the young man in question. We will no doubt know much more when we meet him."

"Very true. We do not know what sort of person he is. He may be a very decent sort of young man, despite everything. I will need your support, Georgie. A man's firm touch may be necessary."

"Of course I will help as much as I can, though I am not so sure about the business of the firm touch. I don't think that's something I will be very good at." He paused. "And on a different note, I have some news. Guess."

"Diva's Paddy has been sick again?"

"No, no. Major Benjy was seen in town today, doing the marketing."

"With Elizabeth?"

"No, just the Major."

"And what did he buy?"

"As far as I could tell, nothing out of the ordinary. Diva saw him going into Twemlow's, and I saw him coming out of Twistevant's, but Evie Bartlett saw him entering the Trader's Arms."

"Now why would he be going there?" Lucia asked. She smiled. "I think we may be able to guess, can we not?"

"But why he and not Elizabeth? To do the marketing, I mean, not the Trader's Arms."

"I confess that is a puzzle," Lucia admitted.

"Perhaps she is ill?" Georgie suggested.

"I think it more likely that she has sent Benjy

as a kind of – what is the word? – an advance scouting party. In fact, I am sure that is it. If he makes a satisfactory report back to Grebe, take my word for it that we will see Elizabeth tomorrow, or some time very soon."

"Which means…?"

"I believe it possible that this signifies a return to Tilling life by the Mapp-Flints."

"Well, that will be a nice change," Georgie said. "Why, it's been nearly impossible to organise bridge parties without them."

"Poor Elizabeth," said Lucia. "She must be feeling lonely all on her own at Grebe, with only Major Benjy for company." She sighed in a sympathetic manner, but there was also an element of satisfaction in the sigh, which would have gone unnoticed by anyone who was less familiar with her moods than Georgie.

"I think we will see her in town tomorrow," Georgie said. "Either doing her marketing, or taking tea at Diva's."

"Did Major Benjy speak to anyone, do you know?"

"He said Hello to me, but no more, and Diva didn't say whether he'd spoken to her."

"And I am sure dear Diva would have let you know if he had," said Lucia. "We may take it, therefore, that he did not."

"Well, we will see, won't we?"

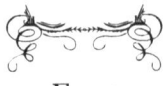

Five

The next day saw the streets of Tilling graced by the presence of Elizabeth Mapp-Flint, bearing her marketing basket on her arm, and proceeding from shop to shop as if there had been no interruption to her daily routine.

As she came out of Hopkins, the fishmonger's, she almost collided with Diva, who was passing by at her customary speed on her way to the butcher's.

The two ladies stopped, and looked at each other. Both appeared to be unwilling to be the first to break the silence. It seemed that Diva was on the point of turning away, when Elizabeth spoke.

"Good morning, dear," she smiled. "Doing a little marketing?"

The answer to this was self-evident, Diva's arm being encumbered by a large basket in which there already resided a number of packages, apparently from the grocer's.

"Yes," replied Diva, answering with another question to which the answer was in no doubt, and therefore could in no wise be controversial. "You?"

"Yes," said Elizabeth, and stopped, but then apparently decided to continue. "Withers had a headache this morning and felt unable to come into town this morning. And it's such a beautiful day that I decided I would come into town myself and pop into the shops. Dear Tilling! What a delicious treat to see it once again."

Diva could think of many answers to this pretty little speech, but with a great effort held her tongue on the matter, simply remarking that the morning was forecast to hold the best of the weather, and that showers were predicted for the afternoon. "You should take care to be back at Grebe before the rain starts," she concluded.

"Thank you for your concern, dear," said Elizabeth. "I must get back in time for

FIVE

luncheon. Benjy-boy will give me such a scolding if I am late." She turned, as if to go, but stopped and turned back. "Are you free next Tuesday afternoon. Say three o'clock? Tea, and perhaps a little rubber of bridge?"

Diva nodded wordlessly and then spoke. "Not many visitors. Will close tea shop for that afternoon. Yes, I'm free."

"Then that's settled, then. *Au reservoir.*" Elizabeth fluttered her hand in farewell and set sail once more down the High Street, where she soon met the Padre and Evie.

"God give ye good morrow, Mistress Mapp-Flint," said the Padre. "And where might ye be ganging? Some wee bitty errand, I'll be bound."

Elizabeth saw no good reason to let the Padre know the nature of her marketing, but then there was no good reason for him not to know, and on the basis that it was better for her to tell the truth (at least, the truth as it was interpreted by Elizabeth Mapp-Flint) rather than allowing speculation to run its course, she answered that she was going to the stationer's. The truth was that she was planning a visit to the haberdasher's for the purpose of making some rather delicate purchases.

She mentally counted on her fingers. She and Benjy, dear Diva, the Padre and Evie – that was five. "Tuesday. Three o'clock. Tea and a little rubber afterwards?" she suggested.

"That would be lovely," Evie squeaked. "Are we free then, Kenneth?"

"Aye, I ween that we are," he answered. "Muckle kind of ye, Mistress."

There were now three places left if there were to be two tables. The Wyses, or Lucia and Georgie? That left space for one more, which would have to be Irene, though the quaint one's tongue was a weapon against which one had to be constantly on guard. Much as it grieved Elizabeth, she decided on Lucia and Georgie. Mr Wyse's presence at bridge parties was an undeniable, if unintentional, damper on the passions and high drama that accompanied Tilling bridge, and added the spice that made the game worth playing.

Try as hard as she might, for nearly twenty minutes she found it impossible to accidentally meet Lucia or her husband, but at the end of this time her patience was rewarded, as she spotted them coming along the street, and hurried towards the couple.

They halted in their tracks as she approached, and stood still. Clearly it was up to Elizabeth to make the first move.

"Good morning, dear Lucia and Mr Georgie,"

she smiled at them, displaying a large expanse of gleaming white teeth. "What a beautiful morning. And our lovely Tilling so busy and bustling."

"So nice to see you again, dear Elizabeth," said Lucia. "How wonderful to see the inhabitants of Grebe with us once again. And was it Major Mapp-Flint that we saw going into the Trader's Arms yesterday?"

Elizabeth, who had more than a suspicion that Major Benjy had refreshed himself at the Trader's Arms on the previous day, was now having second and third thoughts about the seventh and eighth members of her bridge party. Reluctantly she decided (for she could not be sure of meeting Mr Wyse or Susan on that day) that Lucia and Georgie would have to make up the numbers. "No doubt you did see Benjy-boy going in there to buy a little bottle of Marsala wine. So useful in so many recipes."

Lucia, who was well aware of the presence of Marsala wine in the production of lobster *à la Riseholme*, smiled thinly. "Of course, dear."

There was a short silence, which was broken by a remark of Georgie's on the probability of rain that afternoon.

"What a coincidence," said Elizabeth. "Dear Diva was saying the same thing only a few minutes ago." She paused. Should she or shouldn't she? The thought of Susan's odious MBE and that vulgar Royce polluting the air of Grebe decided her. "Tuesday afternoon. Tea, and perhaps a little rubber of bridge afterwards? Perhaps you can pop in? Do say yes."

Lucia was on the point of accepting this surprising invitation, when Georgie tugged at her sleeve and whispered a few words in her ear. Her face, which had been wearing an anticipatory smile, changed to an expression of regret. "So sorry, dear, but Georgie reminds me that we should be staying at home that afternoon." She fell silent, and Elizabeth stood, mouth slightly agape, with an expression almost like that of a fledgling blackbird expecting the gift of a worm from its parent, as she awaited a further explanation.

None appeared to be forthcoming, however, and Elizabeth pasted a patently false bright smile over her supposed disappointment. "Such a pity. Some other time?"

"Indeed," said Lucia. "Come, Georgie, we must be away."

"*Au reservoir*," Elizabeth half-muttered in a tone that Lucia, had she bothered to do so, would have had to strain her ears to catch. The thought of cancelling, or at least postponing

Five

the tea-party, preferably at the last minute, crossed her mind, but she rejected it – the desire to put her finger on the pulse of Tilling was too strong. She realised that she would have to ask the Wyses to make up the number.

There was no chance of her being able to telephone the invitation, and she was preparing herself to walk to the Wyses' house and face Figgis, Mr Wyse's somewhat intimidating butler, when she spotted Mr Wyse himself on the other side of the road.

"Dear Mr Wyse," she smiled at him as he removed his hat and made a bow to her.

"My dear Mrs Mapp-Flint," he answered her. "May I be permitted to tell you how happy I am to see you in the streets of Tilling once more. Delightful."

This was not a topic of conversation that she was anxious to pursue, and she waved it away with a gesture. "Mr Wyse, how very kind of you to say so. How very opportune that I have met you in this way. I was just on my way to your house to tell you that I would very much appreciate your and Susan's coming to tea at Grebe, with bridge to follow."

"That sounds a most charming plan, and I am sure that Susan will join me in accepting your kind invitation with the greatest of pleasure. When is this entertainment to take place?"

"Next Tuesday afternoon."

The face of Mr Wyse, who had meanwhile pulled a small memorandum book from his pocket, and was examining it, fell. "Alas, dear lady. Tuesday is the one day next week when it will be impossible for us to accept your hospitality."

"Than on another occasion, perhaps?" suggested Elizabeth.

"Certainly," Mr Wyse replied, and after another bow, replaced his hat as they parted.

So, Elizabeth mused to herself, both the Wyses and Lucia and Georgie (she still found it hard to refer to them collectively as "the Pillsons") were engaged on Tuesday. Was this a matter of mere chance? She did not believe in coincidences, and believed, like some ancient philosophers, that all things were connected.

However, connected as these matters might be, tracing the threads that connected them might prove somewhat difficult. Of more urgency was the fact that there were now to be five for her tea-party (she had abandoned the idea of inviting Irene immediately on hearing Mr Wyse's refusal), which meant that Benjy-boy would have to sit out the rubber – as hostess,

Hugh Ashton – 53

Five

she herself could not possibly be expected to do so. There was the risk, she considered, that her husband might discover some hitherto hidden store of whisky or some other alcoholic liquor and take advantage of Elizabeth's interest in the card-table to make use of this discovery, but the advantages of re-entering Tilling society and becoming party to the latest news would outweigh this.

She finished the few errands that remained, and returned to Grebe, racking her brains as to the nature of the mysterious events that would be occurring on Tuesday.

Six

Tuesday at Mallards saw Georgie and Lucia eating their breakfast in a somewhat distracted fashion. An observer would have conjectured (correctly) that they were both preoccupied with the unknown guest who was due to cross their threshold later that day.

Georgie was just buttering a piece of toast preparatory to spreading it with the Gentleman's Relish that formed an invariable part of his breakfasts, when the front door bell rang.

"Goodness!" exclaimed Lucia. "Surely they cannot be here already!"

Happily, she was mistaken, as Grosvenor entered to inform them that Mr Wyse had called.

"Ask him to wait in the garden-room, please,

Six

and inform him that we will be with him in a few minutes."

Georgie rapidly disposed of his toast, and gulped down his coffee, slightly scalding his throat in his haste, as Lucia did the same, before making their way into the garden-room.

"My sincere apologies," Mr Wyse said to them by way of greeting, as he bowed to them in the most polite and charming manner. "This is an unconscionably early hour to pay a visit, but I thought it best to inform you as soon as I could regarding the arrival of Isabel and her friend."

Lucia thanked him, and he continued. "We have just received a telegram from Dover informing us that Isabel and her Italian expect to arrive at Tilling station at forty-three minutes past two this afternoon. They are travelling from Dover to London this morning, and will take breakfast" (the term by which Mr Wyse, in his affected fashion, habitually referred to luncheon) "in Town before travelling to Tilling. Susan's Royce will meet them at the station, and convey Isabel to our house, and, with your permission, will bring this Paolo and his effects here. I trust this arrangement meets with your approval."

"That will be perfectly satisfactory," Lucia told him. "The bedroom is all ready for him, and we are looking forward to our guest's arrival, are we not, Georgie?"

"Indeed," replied her husband, but there was an element of enthusiasm lacking in his voice.

"Excellent," Mr Wyse told her. "Once more, may I offer my and Susan's sincere gratitude for your hospitality towards this stranger in our midst."

When he had left, Lucia turned to Georgie. "Is oo worried?" she asked him. "Oo not looking forward to ickle *Italiano*? Second thoughts?"

"I don't know," he replied, flustered. "My bibelots. Will they be safe? Will *we* be safe? One hears such things about these people."

"Now then, Georgie," Lucia hastened to reassure him. "I am confident this Paolo will be perfectly respectable, regardless of his origins. After all, however eccentric dear Isabel may have been in her behaviour when she was living in Tilling, she has been brought up to be a judge of character, I am sure."

"Even so," said Georgie, "I will hide my bibelots and replace them with my second-best bibelots from the bottom bureau drawer. You should place your jewellery in the safe-deposit box in the bank. And I would advise Grosvenor to hide the plate. I do not think we can be too careful when it comes to this sort of person."

"I think you are worrying too much, my dear," Lucia told him. "There will be time enough to judge."

"Even so, I think we should take precautions," Georgie told her miserably, and made his way upstairs to conceal the treasures in his sitting-room. Lucia, for her part, thought it prudent to at least partially follow Georgie's advice, and removed her more valuable pieces to a drawer, where they lay covered by a pile of unmentionables. As for the plate, to her way of thinking, it was somewhat old-fashioned and ugly, and since it was insured, she would welcome, rather than mourn, its absence should it take it into its head to disappear from Mallards.

These activities took them to lunch. Georgie had attempted a little practice on his piano, but had found it impossible to concentrate. Even his petit point, which usually acted as a sedative, failed to have its usual effect, and he pricked his finger quite severely with his needle, forcing him to drop the cushion cover on which he was working for fear of contaminating it with his blood.

Following lunch, eaten in nervous near-silence, Lucia and Georgie moved into the garden-room, where they stood by the window, scanning the street for Susan's Royce. At length the car made its ponderous way up the street, and Lucia discreetly craned her neck to observe the occupants.

"It's Isabel," she whispered excitedly. "As brown as ever she was – the Italian sun, I suppose – and her hair is a little improved since we last saw her here. The Contessa's influence, perhaps?"

"And the Italian?"

"I cannot see his face, but he appears to be well-enough dressed. Tall, slim... Ah, he is taking his own luggage from the car. Very decent sort of suitcases, I must say."

"No doubt Isabel is responsible for them?"

"No doubt. And he is just about to ring the bell. Let us be ready to receive him." She twitched the curtain shut, and she and Georgie settled into their armchairs, ready to be discovered by Grosvenor and their guest in attitudes of nonchalant idleness.

As Grosvenor showed the visitor into the room and Lucia rose from her chair to welcome him, she, together with the young Italian, seemed turned to stone as they gazed at each other and amazed recognition showed in both their faces.

"Paolo!" exclaimed Lucia in tones of wonder.

"*Lucia mia!*" came the reply.

Six

Georgie, for his part, stood in shocked surprise. "How..? What..?" he stammered.

"We know each other," said Lucia simply. "Paolo was on the cod fishing boat that took Elizabeth and me from the kitchen table and carried us to the Gallagher Banks." She turned to her guest. "*Paolo, come stai?*" she asked him.

"*Molto bene,*" he smiled. "Very good," he added in accented English. "*Molto* happy to see you, Mrs Lucia."

"You speak English now?" Lucia asked in surprise.

"Little only. *Poco.* Isabella teach me some."

"*Bravo,*" Lucia told him. "This," indicating Georgie, "is my husband, Georgie. *Mio marito.*"

"Pleased to meet you, Paolo," Georgie told him.

"I too. Pleased to meet you."

Paolo was about as tall as Georgie, and a little slimmer. His hand, when Georgie shook it, was not as hard as Georgie had expected a fisherman's hand to be, and his clothes, though not of English cut, nevertheless appeared to be of good quality. This again was a little unexpected, given what Georgie and Lucia had been told. His face seemed to Georgie to be honest, but Georgie had to remind himself that first appearances can sometimes be deceiving.

"Paolo," Lucia said, with what sounded like a note of relief in her voice that he would not have to be addressed solely in Italian. "I think that Grosvenor is now ready to show you to your room. *Vostra stanza.*"

"*Grazie.*"

"Well!" said Georgie as the garden-room door closed. "Fancy your knowing him! Who would ever believe such a thing?"

"It does seem like Fate, doesn't it?" Lucia agreed. "He was one of the kindest men on the boat, to Elizabeth as well as to me. And his Italian was not that coarse Neapolitan dialect that the other sailors used, so we spent some time talking to each other." She sighed. "Those days, Georgie. We were often wet and cold, and I missed you, and Tilling, so much, but it was sometimes almost wonderful. Seeing the sun come up in the morning, making its way through the mist, or the sight of the lights of the other boats in the fleet shining through the night under the stars, were some of the most moving experiences of my life." She sighed. "If I had had my paints and brushes with me, I would have attempted to capture those moments on paper, but I do not think I would have been able to do them justice."

Georgie, who had never before heard Lucia

Six

talk about her experiences in this way, was somewhat taken aback, but put it down to the sudden appearance of this Italian fisherman. For, as Georgie had observed, Paolo was indeed a young man, and no mere boy, and a remarkably good-looking young man (albeit in the Mediterranean fashion) at that. He could not help wondering what the Wyses would make of Paolo when they met him. Certainly the fact that he seemed to speak a little English, and understand some more, would be a point in his favour, as would his general appearance and manner, which did not at all correspond to the picture that Georgie had built up in his mind.

"I never realised that your voyage had made such an impression on you," he said.

"Oh, but Georgie, when one has lived through such an experience as that which Elizabeth and I underwent, it can never leave one. Why, I remember that psychoanalyst who once gave a lecture in London that Pepino and I attended – Professor Bonstetter was his name, if I recall rightly – talked about experiences which leave such a mark on one's soul. I am willing to believe that he would never have even begun to imagine such an experience as we went through. It is no wonder that my mind will always remember it."

"I am sure it will," said Georgie. "Quite enough to make anyone remember it. What are we to do with this Paolo? I am glad that he can understand and speak some English. And as you say, his Italian seems to be quite pure – at least I could understand what he was saying, I think."

"Then you have just decided for us what we will do," said Lucia. "We will teach him English, and he can assist us with our Italian. It will be much better for us to learn from a real live Italian, rather than from a book, and for him, when he returns to Italy, he will have another language. Maybe he can find himself a new occupation guiding English tourists, and we will have done him a favour. And who knows?" Lucia went on. "Maybe we can earn our daily bread by guiding Italian visitors around Tilling."

Georgie laughed. "We might be a long time between crusts," he said. "There have not been many such visitors recently."

Lucia chose not to acknowledge this, but carried on as if Georgie had not spoken. "And just imagine – being able to read Dante without a dictionary."

"Or to speak to the Contessa in Italian without anyone else being able to understand a word," Georgie said, excitedly. "How long do you think that Paolo will be staying with us, though? Long enough for us to be able to read Dante?"

"I suppose," said Lucia thoughtfully, "that it all depends on how long it takes for the Wyses to decide that he is an unsuitable son-in-law."

Seven

At Grebe, the afternoon was proceeding as anticipated. Major Benjy had been told by his wife that he did not, in fact, want a rubber of bridge, and that he was to sit out, and fetch and carry cups of tea, small chocolate cakes, cream scones, and such other refreshments and necessities as the three ladies and the Padre might from time to time require.

The first rubber, with Elizabeth partnering the Padre, ended in a rout. Elizabeth had revoked twice, and missed an obvious finesse when the Padre was dummy.

"Eh, that's a sair sight," said her partner, looking at the score sheet. "You're going to have to

Seven

do a mite better than that in the next rubber, my lassie."

Elizabeth, who intensely disliked being called "my lassie", said nothing, but glowered at her husband, while ostentatiously rattling her empty teacup on her saucer.

"Ah, yes, there you are, Liz," he said, in somewhat vague tones as he took her cup and refilled it from the large teapot standing on the side. He was kept busy for the next few minutes refilling the cups and plates of the others, following which he retired to an armchair with his large teacup, from which he could be seen imbibing as the second rubber started.

This time it was Diva who was Elizabeth's partner. She revoked, and despite her protestations, the penalty was applied, and she and Elizabeth paid Evie and the Padre at the end of the rubber.

"I don't know how you could have overlooked that spade, dear," Elizabeth said to Diva as they settled the score. "So useful for change," she remarked absently, as she counted out the pennies before handing them to Evie.

"Probably in the same way that you overlooked that six of clubs and the three of diamonds in the last rubber," Diva answered through clenched teeth.

To this, there was no satisfactory answer, and Elizabeth ruefully calculated that the afternoon's play had cost her one shilling and threepence. There were enough potted meat sandwiches and small chocolate cakes left over to make a satisfactory 'tray' for herself and Major Benjy, if a Welsh rabbit was added, which was a small relief.

"Did ye not ask Mistress Pillson and her mannie?" asked the Padre.

"Or Susan and Algernon?" Evie added.

"I asked Lucia and Georgie, certainly, and the Wyses," Elizabeth answered. She dropped her voice as she continued, "But there is something most mysterious going on. Both of them said that they were engaged this afternoon."

"Coincidence," said Diva. "Lots of people are busy on Tuesdays. Lucky I could was able to come here this afternoon."

"You may call it lucky," Elizabeth said, her mind still running on the revoke.

"I will call it whatever I like," said Diva. "Maybe I should have revoked twice, then we would both be equally lucky."

Elizabeth opened her mouth and was about to deliver a withering retort when she remembered that firstly, the Padre was present, and that some of the words and phrases she proposed to deliver might be interpreted as un-Christian; and secondly, if she and Benjy-boy were to re-take their places in Tilling society, she should keep on friendly terms, if only on the surface, with the others.

She smiled her great smile. "How deliciously droll, dear. Fancy! A contest to see who can revoke most often in a rubber."

"Not what I meant at all," said Diva crossly, but she found herself addressing Elizabeth's back, as Elizabeth had turned to bid farewell to the Padre and Evie.

Eight

The afternoon at Mallards started pleasantly enough. The weather was still warm enough for Lucia and Georgie to conduct Paolo around the garden, with Lucia pointing out to their visitor the names of the flowers and trees in English, and receiving the Italian in reply.

They had reached Lucia's *giardino segreto* (a phrase that Lucia obligingly translated for Paolo), when Foljambe came out of the house towards them, a piece of paper clutched in her hand.

"A telegram for you, sir," she said to Georgie.

Georgie thanked her and took the message from her, and carefully opened the envelope

Eight

with his pearl-handled penknife. His face changed.

"There has been an accident," he informed Lucia. "My sister Ursy."

"A serious accident?" Lucia asked.

"It doesn't say. Tarsome. It simply says— here, read it."

He passed the paper over to Lucia, who read out, "'Ursy accident. Come at once. Say what train. Love Hermy.' Georgie, you must go to your sister."

"But I cannot go tonight – I must have all my things ready. Foljambe," he addressed her, "please prepare my things for a few days' stay."

"Shall I be coming with you, sir?" Foljambe asked him.

Georgie considered this for a minute. Life without Foljambe could be very tarsome, but he considered the extra work that taking Foljambe with him would make for Hermy, and there was also Cadman's happiness to consider (for Georgie had a kind heart). "No, I shall be travelling alone by train. I shall go in and look up the trains for tomorrow morning and then write my reply."

This was something of a sacrifice on Georgie's part. He was always anxious when travelling by train. He might be forced to share his compartment with a disagreeable stranger who would insist on making conversation, or a baby, or another such unpleasant and unwelcome personage. Then there was the worry of his luggage. He could never be certain that all his cases would arrive at the same station as he himself, especially when he was forced to change trains. He remembered one occasion when his dressing case had made its way to Tillingham, a hamlet in Essex, rather than Tilling, on his return from a visit to the West Country where he had gone for a course of strengthening sea-baths and wholesome seaside air.

On consulting the timetable, he found that there was a train that left Tilling at half-past eight, and, if he took a taxi to Waterloo station, and another when he reached Wiltshire, would allow him to be at Ursy's side before midday. He therefore wrote on half a sheet of notepaper, 'Trust accident not serious. Will be with you tomorrow before 12. Love to both Georgie', and gave it to Foljambe to be sent from the post office.

The effort of this, and the anxious anticipation of the next day's train journey, made him feel a little unwell, and he was forced to lie down on the sofa in his sitting-room for a while

Eight

to compose himself. He was awakened by the entrance of Foljambe, who entered the room to inform him of her preparations.

"I've sent off the telegram, sir, and packed everything up for you in two cases, and laid out your things for tomorrow as well as your dinner suit," she told him. "I expect you'll have left the house by the time I come in, so I'd just like to say that Cadman and I hope that your sister will recover soon, and that you have a good journey."

"Thank you, Foljambe."

When he came downstairs for dinner, he discovered Lucia and Paolo engaged, as far as he could tell, in reminiscences about Lucia's travels on the fishing boat. As he stood in the doorway of the garden-room and watched them conversing, he felt an irrational stab of jealousy. He knew that Lucia's affections lay with him, and no other, and felt secure in that knowledge. At the same time, he was disturbed to see Lucia so animated and cheerful in a manner that he had hardly, if ever, observed in her relations with him.

However, as he stepped forward, and the others became aware of his presence, there was no obvious change in their mood, or in their conversation, but Lucia moved a little to one side, making room for him to sit between her and Paolo.

"I very happy here in this house," Paolo told Georgie. "*Signora* Lucia and I have many things to remember."

Georgie told him in return that he was very happy to hear that news, and turned to Lucia.

"Are you rested, Georgie?" Lucia asked him. "And ready for the journey tomorrow? Cadman will drive you to the station, of course."

"Thank you," said Georgie miserably. "I hope that I won't have to stay too long away from you and from Tilling."

Dinner was a rather subdued affair. Despite Lucia's attempts to inject an Italian atmosphere of sunshine with the introduction of a dish of macaroni and tomatoes and a bottle of Chianti wine to accompany it, Georgie's mood remained resolutely English and overcast.

"I will have an early night tonight," he told Lucia.

"Of course, dear," said Lucia. "Sleep well."

As he had feared, Georgie did not sleep at all well. The macaroni did not sit easily in his stomach, and somehow the train in his dream miraculously turned into a cross-Channel steamer pitching and rolling its way to France.

He awoke in good time to eat a light breakfast

EIGHT

before bidding Lucia a fond farewell and setting off with Cadman to the station. Much to his relief, the journey proceeded smoothly, and he arrived, with all his luggage, at the cottage where Hermy and Ursy lived and moved and had their being.

"Glad to see you, Georgie," said Hermy as she opened the door to him. "Thanks for coming." Much to Georgie's surprise, her usual jaunty air did not seem to have deserted her. "Ursy's in the back room, silly thing."

"What's happened?" asked Georgie.

Hermy laughed. "Bit of a lark, really. She tried to jump her bicycle across a ditch yesterday, and didn't manage it. We thought her neck was broken."

"And is it?" Georgie was horrified. He was fond of his sisters, as noisy and as unlike him in almost every way as they might be, and though he very much disliked injuries and illnesses, at least when they were not his own, he felt glad that he had done his duty as a brother by visiting her.

Hermy shook her head. "The doctor came round and told us that she had simply jarred her spine, and she was to stay in bed for a week or so."

"So I've come here for nothing? I mean... It's

all very nice to see you, but..." Georgie was annoyed that he had spent all this time and effort for what had turned out to be a relatively minor accident.

"By the time old fusspot Doctor Hilton had made up his mind what was wrong with Ursy, we'd sent that telegram to you, and you'd already replied telling us that you were coming, bless you. So we decided, Ursy and me, that it would be nice to see you, anyway." She examined her brother critically. "And how's married life, then, brother?" She poked him in the waistcoat with a pointed finger. "Treating you well, I see." She laughed, a trifle coarsely.

"Well..."

"Come on, let's go and see Ursy. I'll put the kettle on and we can have a cup of tea and a bun and chat away."

Nine

Despite her public protestation that the absence of the two couples at Elizabeth's tea was a mere coincidence, Diva had failed to convince herself of her own words. Accordingly, she set out the next day to do her marketing in Tilling by a route that took her past the Wyses' house, but, try as she might, she could see nothing through the windows that gave her any indication of the absence of the couple the previous day.

She bought her groceries and made up her mind to go past Mallards, since she had drawn a blank at the Wyses'. If she went carefully up the far side of the road, it was just possible to see into the garden-room, where Lucia might be sitting, in order to gain some understanding of the mystery which now seemed to surround Mallards and Porpoise Street. That mystery had assumed new depths only a few minutes previously when Evie, who had been forced to visit the coal-merchant near the station early that morning, owing to the church stoves having consumed a greater quantity of coal than expected earlier in the week, had informed her (Diva) that she (Evie) had observed Georgie Pillson getting out of the car and presumably taking the train to London.

"And he had a lot of luggage with him," Evie had said, excitedly. "At least two cases and a hat-case. More than he'd need for a day trip, anyway. He's going away for a bit."

"Have they quarrelled?" Diva had wondered aloud, 'they' in this case obviously being Lucia and Georgie.

"Maybe," Evie had told her, standing still as a thought had occurred to her. "Maybe he's gone to stay with that opera singer, Olga something? He went to stay with her in France once, you know. I'm sure I don't know what I'd think if Kenneth ever did something like that."

"I'm sure the Padre would never dream of doing such a thing," Diva had told her,

Nine

loyally. "Now if it were Major Benjy we were discussing—"

Both ladies had then stopped suddenly, aware that they might be entering territory that was best left unexplored.

"Anyway," Evie had informed Diva, breaking the silence, "I thought I might go and visit Lucia. I might be able to cheer her up."

Diva, well aware that the ultimate beneficiary of Evie's plan was not to be Lucia, but Evie herself, who would thereby be the first to know of the reasons behind Georgie's disappearance, had shaken her head.

"Much better not to," she had said emphatically. "Sleeping dogs lying and all that."

"So you think there might be something going on after all?" Evie had asked.

"Probably not. Storm in a teacup," Diva had answered. "We'll know soon enough anyway. We always do." And with Evie's ambition to be first with the news now firmly crushed, she had strode off, deep in thought, and determined to find an excuse to pass Mallards.

As she had surmised, it was just possible for Diva to see through the garden-room window. And as she had hoped, Lucia was clearly visible in the garden-room, talking to someone who was invisible from where Diva was standing. If

Diva stood on tiptoe, she would just about be able to make out who it was... She looked in all directions to ensure that she was unobserved, and contorted herself into a position where she could make out quaint Irene Coles, seemingly in conversation with Lucia and... Wriggle and contort herself as she might, Diva was unable to make out this unknown personage, but from the little she could see, they appeared to be wearing trousers, rather than a skirt, and might therefore be presumed to be male. Not the Padre, to be sure, or Evie would no doubt have known about it, and Georgie was clearly not a candidate, having taken the train to wherever it might prove to be. The little of the pattern of the trousers that Diva had seen made it unlikely that Major Benjy was the wearer of these garments. If she had not seen Mr Wyse entering his house as she turned the corner on her way to Mallards, she might have suspected him, but it was too frustrating not to know.

Of course, it might be a friend of Irene's, who shared her penchant for masculine garb, and whom Irene had invited to meet her friend Lucia, but that would seem less likely. As far as Diva was aware, Irene had never had a friend to visit her at Tilling, and she could think of no reason why that situation should have changed.

Hugh Ashton – 59

NINE

There was one other piece of news that Janet had mentioned the previous evening, but the excitement of the bridge rubber had driven it out of her head until now. Janet had said that she had seen the Wyses' Royce motor stop at Mallards. As to who was in the car, or whether someone had entered or left Mallards, she "couldn't say". But this was obviously (obvious, that is, to a trained observer of Tilling life, such as Diva) connected with the mysterious errands of the Wyses and of the Pillsons that had prevented them from enjoying their bridge the previous day.

Try as she might, Diva was no nearer being able to view the inhabitants of the garden-room with any clarity, and she turned away somewhat baffled and disappointed not to have unravelled the mystery.

On her way home she encountered Elizabeth Mapp-Flint, who greeted her with a wide smile.

"Dear Diva, such a lovely bridge-party yesterday, was it not? The loss of a few pennies is surely nothing when set against the company of a few dear friends."

Diva, whose feelings as regards pecuniary loss were a little stronger, particularly as she had closed her tea-rooms for the afternoon in order to go to Grebe, held her peace.

"And," Elizabeth went on, seemingly determined to ignore Diva's silence, "what about the news concerning Mr Georgie?"

"Heard it. Evie told me."

"But what are we to make of it? Dashing off to see that Olga Braceley, and leaving poor Lucia all alone."

"Now then, who said he was going to see Olga Braceley? That's pure supposition on your part, and you know it, Elizabeth."

"Well, I don't know where else he might have gone without Lucia."

"There was that time when he went away to the seaside by himself and Lucia caught influenza and you were convinced that she couldn't speak Italian, and the Contessa got that letter from her in perfect Italian," Diva reminded her.

"That was some sort of conjuring trick. I don't know how she managed it, but I still don't believe she can speak Italian, any more than you and I can speak Chinese. And anyway," Elizabeth continued, aware that she was skating on thin ice, "even if Mr Georgie did go away by himself that time, he went to France to stay with that prima donna that other time, didn't he? And poor dear Lucia looked, oh so careworn and downcast at that time."

NINE

Diva responded with what might uncharitably have been described as a snort.

"You may scoff," said Elizabeth, acutely aware of the meaning contained within Diva's snort, "but did we ever find out the true story of all that business?" She stopped, aware that she could not afford to alienate potential allies, and gave a little laugh. "But it is not for us to pry and meddle in others' affairs, is it?"

To which, there was no satisfactory answer that Diva could give without provoking a breach of the uneasy peace that now seemed to prevail, and the two ladies parted company, with a good deal of dissatisfaction and grievance for past actions divided equally between them.

Ten

As Diva had seen through the window of the garden-room, Irene Coles had taken it upon herself to visit Lucia, with no specific object in mind, other than the fact that she was waiting for the paint to dry on her latest canvas, and was bored with her own company.

Grosvenor, having received no instructions to the contrary, had admitted her to the garden-room, where she beheld Lucia in conversation with a strange man. Lucia looked startled to see Irene, clearly not having expected any visitors.

"Dear one," Irene exclaimed as she entered and kissed Lucia on the cheek, "who is your

Ten

friend?" She regarded Paolo (for it was he) with an approving eye.

"This is Signor Paolo Alberghi from Italy, who is staying with us at the moment," Lucia informed her. She felt under no compulsion to provide Irene, at least at this stage, with any further information.

"Pleased to meet you," Irene said to Paolo, who had risen from his chair and bowed to her. She made a show of looking around the room. "And where is Georgie?" she asked Lucia. There were quite clearly other questions burning in her mind, but this one was possibly the one she felt safest to ask at this time.

"One of his sisters has suffered some sort of accident," Lucia explained. "He received a telegram yesterday and took the train this morning. He will probably be away for a few days."

"I see," said Irene. She turned towards Paolo. "How long are you staying in Tilling?" she asked him.

"Two week, maybe three, maybe four," he answered with a shrug. "Sorry, *signora*, I not speak English good," he told her.

"Oh good," said Irene. "Paolo, may I see your hand, please?"

To Paolo's seeming embarrassment, she took his hand in hers, and examined it critically.

"Yes, that's a good hand. May I see your arm?" she asked, pointing to her own arm, and rolling up her sleeve to show him what she meant.

She assisted him in unbuttoning his cuff, and examined his forearm. "Superb," she exclaimed, and stepped back, examining his head from a number of different angles. "Lucia, may I borrow him, please? If the rest of him is half as good as what I have seen just now, he will serve as an excellent model for my next masterpiece."

Lucia smiled. "Paolo is a free man," she answered. "He is not my property."

"Can you please explain to him in Italian what I want. Explain that he's quite safe with me, and I'll give him back to you, as good as new. And he won't catch cold, even if he does have to take all his clothes off. I have a new oil-stove in my studio, especially for this sort of occasion. And tell him that I'll pay him something for his trouble, of course."

"Later, dear Irene," Lucia smiled, though inwardly she was wondering what the Italian words might be for all of this. "It might be a trifle, shall we say, embarrassing for me to explain all this to him in front of you. I will be able to give you an answer this afternoon."

"Oh, very well," said Irene, and proceeded to

TEN

pull out a sketchpad and pencil from one of her voluminous pockets, which she used to make a sketch of Paolo's face. "There," she exclaimed after a few minutes. "That's the sort of face I need for my picture." She held the drawing up for examination by Lucia and Paolo. The latter looked at it, and exclaimed, "*Magnifico, signora*! It is wonderful!" And before Irene realised what was happening, he had moved forward and kissed her on both cheeks.

"Well, I didn't expect *that*!" said Irene, stepping back hurriedly. "But make it clear to him, Lucia, that this is the last time something like that happens. I'm off. Send him round this afternoon if he agrees, otherwise just drop a note in at the door, and it will have to be Hopkins from the fish shop again."

She departed, and Lucia, as so often was the case with Irene, was left with the feeling that she had been visited by a small, but particularly energetic, whirlwind.

With the aid of an Italian dictionary, and some simple Italian and English phrases, she was able to convey Irene's request to Paolo, who received the proposition with every indication of interest, and announced that he would act as a model for the '*bella signora*' at any time. Lucia, who would not have thought of applying that adjective to Irene, could only wonder at the strange tricks that could be played by emotions.

"*È sposita?*" he asked, and Lucia was forced to tell him that Irene was unmarried, and strained her Italian to the utmost to convey the idea that in her opinion, Irene's marrying was as unlikely as a hippopotamus to be discovered disporting itself in the garden.

It was clear at lunch that Paolo was very much taken with the idea of being an artist's model. Lucia, with the utmost delicacy, had given strong indications that he might be required to remove at least part of his clothing, but this seemed to be a matter of some indifference to him, which Lucia ascribed to his Mediterranean upbringing.

After lunch, she went out into the road, and ensured that the streets were empty before going back in, collecting Paolo, and depositing him at Taormina, Irene's cottage.

"Behave yourself," she told him firmly. "*Comportati bene*," she repeated, having previously memorised the phrase, before turning for home.

She met Diva Plaistow as she turned the corner, and could not avoid the question put to her in the form of a declaration.

TEN

"Evie Bartlett says that she saw Mr Georgie at the station this morning," Diva told her.

"Perfectly correct," said Lucia. Seeing that more was expected of her, she added, "He had a telegram last night from one of his sisters, telling him that the other sister had suffered an accident and needed him to visit them in Hampshire."

"Oh dear," said Diva. Some additional force was given to her words by her unspoken regret that there was a perfectly straightforward and innocent explanation for Georgie's absence. "When does he return?"

"He will no doubt send me a telegram as soon as he knows," Lucia answered, a little tartly. She did not really see what business it was of Diva's when Georgie returned to Tilling.

With what she took to be great subtlety, Diva remarked that Lucia must find it somewhat lonely to be at Mallards on her own.

"Not at all, dear Diva. Of course I do not have the great press of people coming in and out, as you do at your little place – those delicious teas of yours – but I manage to keep myself entertained quite easily. My books, you know, my flowers, and my music. And I just came out to post a letter."

Diva did not think it necessary to point out

that the nearest post-box to Mallards lay on the other side of the street, and there was no reason for Lucia to have crossed over to the side where they were both now standing. This sort of detail was of the type that Lucia found it easy to ignore.

"And no visitors?" she asked.

"Quaint Irene paid me a short visit this morning," Lucia laughed. "Full of plans and ideas for her latest painting. Some of her artistic notions are quite shocking, but I hope I have persuaded her that a little more modesty might be in order. I have always maintained that great art does not need to be immodest or shocking to be considered truly great. Take the great Leonardo, for example. His Mona Lisa is one of the finest paintings in the world, and yet there is nothing immodest about it. But tell me," returning to earth, "what of yesterday's bridge? So sorry that we were unable to take part."

"Elizabeth sadly out of practice," Diva told her. "Revoked twice in one rubber. Missed an easy finesse."

"Poor Elizabeth," Lucia replied. "But then we might even say, poor us. No bridge for ever so long, it seems. We must have a good long evening of bridge at Mallards soon. Two tables."

TEN

"That will be nice. Time we all got together again."

"Indeed. *Au reservoir.*"

They parted, leaving Diva's raging curiosity still on the boil. She went back to her tea-room where Janet was just fetching a batch of scones out of the oven. Business was slow at the tea-room that afternoon, and Diva kept "popping out", to use a favourite expression of hers, at regular intervals, leaving Janet in charge. She was convinced that Lucia, though she might have been telling the truth, and nothing but the truth, was certainly not telling the whole truth.

Her persistence was eventually rewarded at the fifth attempt. She was able to observe a young man, unknown to Tilling, departing from Irene's cottage. Though she was too far away to observe his features clearly, it seemed, even from that distance, that he was an exceedingly handsome young man, if a little foreign in appearance.

He turned the corner, and Diva, as if drawn by a magnet, followed to observe his destination. To her complete astonishment, he knocked on the front door of Mallards, where Grosvenor admitted him, and closed the door behind him.

"Well!" Diva said to herself. "Georgie's away,

and Lucia has a young man to visit." She wondered if she had just seen the mysterious owner of the pair of legs she had seen earlier through the garden-room window.

But the day had not yet delivered its full complement of surprises to Diva. When she returned to the tea-room, she found Susan Wyse, swathed in her sables as usual, with a very brown young lady, very smartly dressed, but with most peculiar hair, whom Diva recognised after a short while as Isabel Poppit, who had not been seen in Tilling, at any rate by Diva or any of her friends, for the past six months at the very least. She appeared, for some reason or reasons unknown, to be less than happy. Indeed, her expression was one of a resigned sadness, such as might be seen on the faces of some saints as depicted by Italian medieval artists.

But, drop as many heavy hints as to Isabel's previous whereabouts as she might, as she assiduously plied the Wyse-Poppit's table with the scones, sandwiches, and cakes that comprised the eighteen-penny tea, and passing as often as possible by the table where Isabel and Susan were sitting in the hope of picking up some overheard scraps of conversation, she

TEN

remained ignorant of the reason for Isabel's sudden reappearance in Tilling society.

Eleven

Whoever coined the phrase "ignorance is bliss" had never taken into account the character of Diva Plaistow. As she closed the doors on her tea-room, and watched Susan Wyse and Isabel Poppit enter the Royce, which had been waiting outside the door for the full hour that they had taken to consume their afternoon tea, her curiosity was piqued to the limit. Bliss was as alien to her mind at that moment as was the desire to grow wings and fly.

Could there be, she asked herself as the composed herself to sleep later that night, some connection between Lucia's young man and Isabel? Other than the fact that both the Wyses and the inhabitants of Mallards had both claimed prior engagements on the day of Elizabeth's tea-party, she could think of none. And where, she wondered, had Isabel been? The fact that she was as brown as a nut meant nothing – even when she had most definitely been a resident of Tilling, one of her favourite pastimes on sunny days had been to lie in the sand dunes wearing a distressingly small amount of clothing, an occupation she had referred to as meetings of her 'Browning Society'. Neither did the state of her hair call for any exceptional comment – it had, in the memory of Tilling, and in the opinion of most, charitably been described as 'unruly'.

No, the mystery lay not in Isabel's outward appearance, but to her very appearance in Tilling at all. Neither Susan nor Algernon Wyse had mentioned her very existence for some time. Something, as quaint Irene would have said, was 'up'.

Diva lay awake, and against all her natural instincts, found herself wishing for a conversation with Elizabeth Mapp-Flint, if only to be able to pour cold water on some of Elizabeth's more lurid theories regarding the sudden appearance of these two strangers in Tilling.

The next day, her wish was granted. By

judiciously spinning out her errands, Diva contrived to meet Elizabeth outside Rice's.

"Any news, dear?" Elizabeth asked her. "Benjy-boy and I have been like little church mice for so long, I hardly know what's happening in my own town."

Diva, rather than making the obvious retort that this isolation had been self-imposed, and could have been terminated at any time, informed Elizabeth that Susan Wyse had taken tea in Ye Olde Tea-Shop. "But she was not alone," she added. "Guess who was with her?"

Elizabeth was about to suggest the Archbishop of Canterbury or the Prince of Wales, but held her peace, seeing Diva as a possible future ally in any anticipated conflicts. "I cannot guess, dear," she smiled, displaying her splendid teeth. "You will have to tell poor little me."

"Isabel Poppit," Diva exclaimed with an air of triumph. "Fancy! We haven't seen her for a long time."

"On her motorcycle? With dear Susan riding behind? That must have been a sight to behold." Since this did not malign Diva, Elizabeth felt it safe to allow her sarcasm a little romp on a short leash.

"No. Royce. Stayed outside my tea-shop for

ELEVEN

an hour. Two eighteen-pennies." Diva was telegraphic, not trusting herself to say more.

"Of course, dear. And how did she look? Isabel, I mean."

"Brown. Hair a mess. New clothes. Smart. Didn't look happy though."

"Where has she been?"

"Don't know. Wouldn't say."

"She's been ill with some sort of infectious disease," Elizabeth pronounced. "She's been sent away for a rest-cure, but she's not completely well again."

Diva was forced to agree that this was a possible reason for Isabel Poppit's disappearance and re-appearance, but she still had a trump card to play. "And then there's Lucia's young man," she said, registering with pleasure the look of surprise on Elizabeth's face.

"You mean Mr Georgie?" Elizabeth said. "Not as young as he was, dear, if that's who you're talking about."

"No, no, no," protested Diva. "You know that Georgie's gone to visit— well, we won't go into that, will we? Yesterday I saw a young man – very good-looking he was, too – come out of Irene's house."

"Well, that is a surprise, I agree."

"But that's not the half of it," Diva went on.

"After he left Irene's house, he went straight up the hill to Mallards, rang the bell, and Grosvenor let him straight in."

"And Mr Georgie away. Oh, dearie me," said Elizabeth. "What an age we're living in."

"There's probably some completely innocent explanation," said Diva, in the confident expectation of drawing an unwarranted accusation out of Elizabeth – an accusation that might be stored up, and subsequently used against her at some future date to some effect.

"Of course there is, dear," agreed Elizabeth. "But I'm afraid I'm not clever enough to see it."

"I was wondering whether we might go and call on Lucia," Diva said, hoping that Elizabeth would rise to this additional bait.

"Certainly not," was the answer. "I mean, just imagine if we went there and found..." Her voice trailed off, leaving Diva to imagine for herself what Elizabeth considered might be discovered in the garden-room if an unexpected visit were to be paid. The result, in Diva's mind at least, was enough of a stick with which to beat Elizabeth in the future – for Diva, though as fond of news and gossip as anyone in Tilling, nonetheless did not believe Lucia (or Georgie, for that matter) to be capable of the

Eleven

sort of thing that Elizabeth was hinting at, and Elizabeth obviously did.

She responded as noncommittally as she could manage, and the two parted company. Diva made a point of taking a slightly circuitous route to Mallards, in the hope of seeing something more than the end of a pair of trousers through the window of the garden-room.

She was rewarded, however, by the sight of Elizabeth standing at the same spot where she had stood the day before, contorting herself in an attempt to peer through the garden-room window, but apparently with no success, as she turned away, with Diva managing to conceal herself from Elizabeth's view only just in time to avoid detection.

Twelve

As Diva was looking at Elizabeth's fruitless efforts to discern the inhabitants of the garden-room, Lucia was sitting on a garden-chair, facing Paolo, who was sitting in another. A vase in which Lucia was arranging dahlias stood on a table between them, and it was through this floral screen that they conversed, in a mixture of Italian and English. A small English-Italian dictionary lay on the table next to the vase, to which both Lucia and Paolo had frequent recourse, and the conversation was held in a sometimes halting mixture of English and Italian.

The chief subject of discourse was Paolo's affections, and the object or objects to which

Twelve

they had been, were presently, and should be in the future, directed.

Lucia had been somewhat surprised by Paolo's contention that he found Isabel Poppit to be *bellissima*. Unless she had changed dramatically in the months since Lucia had last seen her, this was not an adjective that Lucia could ever imagine applying to Isabel Poppit. She felt he was on firmer ground when he referred to her as 'amusing', given her reported propensity for collecting spoonerisms and malapropisms.

However, much as he professed, in a dramatic operatic Italian which Lucia found easy to understand the general sense, though the precise details (if any) passed over her head, there had been a change in his world.

For Irene Coles had come into his life. He insisted on describing to the horrified Lucia how he had entered her studio, and immediately she had requested him to remove his garments. Lucia was rapidly losing her Italian at this point, but she took him to be saying that when he was completely unclad, Irene had called in *"una signora molto alta"*, whom Lucia could identify as Lucy, Irene's guardsman-like maid, seemingly to admire him. And so, it appeared, Irene had sketched him.

Twelve

At the end of an hour or so, he had been invited to dress and inspect the artwork on which Irene had been working. "*Magnifico!*" he exclaimed to Lucia. It was, he declared, the equal, if not the superior of any of the paintings in his father's collection.

At this point, Lucia, who had been listening to him in a kind of horrified daze, stopped him, believing that her Italian had once more led her astray. However, a little work with the dictionary soon proved to her that her ears had not deceived her, and he had indeed been referring to a collection of paintings owned by his father.

"But your father..." she began hesitantly. "Is he not a fisherman like you? How does he come to have such paintings?"

Paolo threw back his head and laughed pleasantly. "My father is no more a fisherman than I," he said.

"But... but..." Lucia was hopelessly confused. "You are a fisherman, are you not? I met you on the *Allodola*, did I not?"

Paolo wagged a playful finger at her. "*Lucia mia*," he said. "I *was* a fisherman," he told her, emphasising the English past tense.

"And now you are?"

"I am my father's son," he said simply.

Hugh Ashton – 81

Lucia sighed. "And who is your father?"

"His name is Pietro Alberghi, and he is the richest man in our village, I may say, in our region. He owns twenty, maybe thirty, fishing boats and a factory to preserve the *baccalà*, the cod as you say, and they are sold all over Italy under the name of *Pesce Marino Neapolitan*."

"But you were on the *Allodola*, working as a fisherman?"

"I was told by my father that I should learn from where our family money comes. I made two voyages. One on the *Santo Andreo*, and the second, when you and the other English lady met us on the table, on the *Allodola*."

"And now?"

"I work in my father's office."

Lucia was quiet for a moment. It seemed that Paolo might be more acceptable to the Wyses as a possible son-in-law now that it appeared that he was more than a humble fisherman. However, against this was his evident infatuation with Irene – an infatuation, Lucia was sure, that would lead to disappointment, as she could by no stretch of the imagination envisage Irene accepting Paolo as anything more than a model for her art – and his current corresponding indifference to the charms, such as they were, of Isabel Poppit.

She leaned forward. "Paolo," she said to him, speaking with great earnestness. "Isabel is a good girl." She was a little unsure as to whether that was true or not, but she did not want to see Paolo's waves of passion to beat against the unyielding rocky shore that was Irene Coles. Especially she felt that, now he had declared his family's station in life, a future as son-in-law to the Wyses seemed like a less remote possibility than it had done previously.

"She is a good girl," Paolo agreed. "But she cannot draw or paint."

"That is true, to the best of my knowledge," Lucia admitted.

"And also there is this," Paolo added. "Never has she invited me to take off my clothes in front of her."

Lucia hurriedly changed the subject from this indelicate topic, fearing the depths to which it might lead if explored further. She hastened to enquire of Paolo whether he would prefer tomato or brown Windsor soup with their evening meal. Since a full explanation of brown Windsor soup was beyond her and Paolo's mutual linguistic comprehension, they determined that tomato soup would form the first course of the meal, following which decision Paolo announced his intention to take a short nap.

It was clear to Lucia, though, that her diversionary tactics had not succeeded in taking Paolo's mind off the subject of Irene Coles. She wished that Georgie was with her, for even if he did not always provide a solution to her problems, he very often laid the foundations for a course of action which would lead to the untying of the knot. In any event, this was a problem that needed a man's touch – and though Lucia was willing to declare, together with Queen Elizabeth that she had "the heart and stomach of a man", it was neither a heart nor a stomach that would sway Paolo from his unsuitable obsession.

Her wish was in some way granted when Grosvenor appeared bearing a telegram from Georgie informing Lucia that he would be returning to Tilling on the following afternoon, since his sister's accident was not as serious as had first been imagined.

Thirteen

Elizabeth Mapp-Flint lost little time in informing her husband of what had transpired that morning as they say over their lunch of lukewarm mutton and watery potatoes.

"Of course," she said to him, "Diva Plaistow would have none of it, but it's my opinion that Georgie Pillson, whatever he or Lucia may say, has gone off to see that Braceley woman again."

Major Benjy could only shake his head to this assertion, but it was unclear whether this signified dissent, or whether it was due to the fact that he was at that moment masticating a piece of indigestible mutton-fat.

"And that man at Lucia's that Diva saw going into Mallards," Elizabeth went on. "What

THIRTEEN

she means by having strange young men in the house with her husband away, I don't know. If she was still Mayor, I would feel it to be my civic duty to call a motion of moral censure against her in the Council meeting."

The Major, who by now had disposed of the mutton-fat by fair means or foul, shook his head again, this time in a manner that unequivocally signified dissent from his wife's views. "Well, she's not Mayor any more, Liz," he pointed out, "and I don't think it would be any business of the Council's who she decides to invite to stay with her, whether or not she is Mayor."

"And," his wife continued, seemingly oblivious of his comment, "that Isabel Poppit is back in Tilling again."

"Didn't know she had ever left Tilling," Major Benjy remarked, spearing a carrot with his fork.

"Well, maybe she had not actually left Tiling," Elizabeth conceded. "But no-one had seen her in the town for— oh, such a long time."

"Doesn't mean anything," he objected, in a rather annoyed tone. The carrot was clearly attempting to compensate for the watery nature of the potatoes with its texture, and the Major had experienced some difficulty in cutting and spearing it. "My old friend Captain Puffin, God rest his soul, had those dizzy spells at times, and there were occasions when no-one saw hide nor hair of him for a week. No-one except his cook, that is. And, talking of cooks," he remarked, waving his fork with its cargo of half-raw carrot, "this meal is hardly fit to be eaten."

Elizabeth, who privately shared the same opinion of the food before them, nonetheless felt compelled to defend her domestic staff and all their works. "Perfectly delicious, Benjy-boy. In any case, we should remember those who are unfortunate enough not to be able to eat in the same style as us."

"Lucky beggars," muttered the Major in a voice intended to be *sotto voce*, but which was still audible to his wife, who responded with a scornful sniff.

"And Captain Puffin not being seen for a week except by his cook – and I have always maintained that Mrs Gashly drank, so goodness alone knows what she saw and didn't see – is a very different kettle of fish to Isabel Poppit's having been invisible to all for six months or more. Very different," she repeated emphatically.

"If you say so, Liz," Major Benjy remarked offhandedly. "Poor old Puffin," he mused. "We

Thirteen

may have argued at times, but we had some jolly good evenings together."

Elizabeth, who still remembered with some considerable resentment an occasion when, following one of those jolly good evenings, she had been accused by an inebriated Puffin of herself being drunk – an incident which had led, somewhat indirectly through her decided rejection of the Captain as a potential suitor, to the state of wedded bliss in which she now found herself, expressed her dissent in another eloquent sniff. Despite the wealth of meaning that she had managed to pack into that wordless sound, it managed to pass unnoticed by her husband.

"I want you to visit Lucia," she informed her husband.

"I? Why on earth should I want to do that?" he asked indignantly. "I was going to play a round of golf this afternoon, since the weather has turned out so well."

"I am sorry about your golf, but I am sure the weather will hold till tomorrow," she informed him, without a trace of sympathy in her voice. "You are to go there and ask to borrow that translation of Dante that she offered to lend me last December."

Major Benjy scratched his head. "Why me,

Liz? And why have you left it so late to borrow that book?"

"Because if I go there myself, Lucia will suspect that I am trying to discover her secret, whatever that may be. You may tell her that I have turned my ankle or something along those lines if she asks why I have not visited myself, and that I have only just now had the leisure to take her up on her kind offer to lend me the book."

"I see."

"But of course, you are to find out who that young man staying with her might be, and to discover where Mr Georgie has really gone. Is that clear?" She felt the need to emphasise this, as Benjy-boy had been known to misinterpret her wishes on a number of occasions. One of these, of some standing, came to the forefront of her mind. "And while you are in town, you should pay a visit to Irene Coles, and to discover when she will be free to paint me."

This referred to the disastrous occasion on which Elizabeth had unequivocally (or so she thought) requested a portrait of herself for her fiftieth birthday present. However, the Major had taken her hints as being a demand for a picture of himself, and had therefore commissioned a portrait from Georgie Pillson

Thirteen

– Irene's fees being more than he was prepared to pay – which had met with intense disapproval from his wife. He had therefore been forced into agreeing to ask Irene Coles to create Elizabeth's portrait, and though he had told his wife that he had made his request, which was currently being considered by Irene pending her availability, the truth was that he had been unable to pluck up the courage to do so.

"Oh, very well," he answered her. "But I am sure that the answer will be the same."

Accordingly after lunch he set off for Tilling with a sense of foreboding. His errands of the afternoon demanded more courage and cunning than he presently felt able to summon, even more than on the occasions when he had supposedly faced starving tigers in India.

Fourteen

He decided to make Mallards his first stop, and on being admitted by Grosvenor, was shown to the morning-room where Lucia was practicing the treble part of a Beethoven symphony arranged for four hands.

"Ah, I am sorry to interrupt your music," he began. "I was wondering – that is to say, Liz was wondering..."

"Yes?" said Lucia brightly. "Perhaps there is something I can help with?"

"Yes, indeed. As I was saying, Liz said that you had offered to lend her some book or other. Now, bless my soul, I can't remember which book she said that it was. She would ask you herself, you understand, but she has turned

Fourteen

her ankle and found it impossible to come into town."

Lucia, who had no recollection of such an offer, frowned. "Oh dear, I am so sorry to hear of her accident. How did it happen?"

Major Benjy, whose powers of invention were not of the strongest, other than when far-off and long-ago incidents involving tigers were concerned, was unable to supply an immediate answer, but eventually came up with the explanation that his wife had tripped over the steps leading to the kitchen.

"Oh, that does indeed sound particularly dangerous, Major Benjy," Lucia answered him. "You should have those steps seen to as soon as possible." She paused. "Perhaps I should visit Elizabeth and take the book myself, once we have established which book it is that I promised to lend her."

The Major, who knew what the result of such a visit might be, shook his head vigorously. "No, I must take it myself," he protested. "Perfect quiet and rest, that's the thing for Liz."

"Very well, then," Lucia replied. "But first you must tell me which book it is that I promised. Dear me, I am always lending my books to my friends, and I cannot remember to whom I have promised the loan of which book."

FOURTEEN

Major Benjy racked his brains, and came up with the answer. "Dante," he pronounced. "I believe you have a translation that Liz wanted to study a little before last Christmas, but she has not had the time until now, you understand."

Lucia smote her brow. "Of course!" she cried. "I remember saying how much I had learned from my reading of the *Paradiso*, and dear Elizabeth, having no Italian, I believe, asked me if I had a translation that she could study." She tripped to the bookcase, and returned with a volume in her hand. "I am sure she will enjoy the *Paradiso*, but in her condition, I cannot wholeheartedly recommend the *Inferno* or *Purgatorio*. And any aids I can give her in understanding, I will be happy to impart. She only has to telephone, or I can come to Grebe and we can spend a happy afternoon together with the divine Dante."

Major Benjy, who was well aware that any afternoon in which both Elizabeth and Lucia were together would be far from happy, thanked her for her offer in as noncommittal a tone as he could achieve. "And your husband?" he added, by way of what he took to be a casual afterthought.

"He has been visiting his sisters. One of them sustained some injury in an accident of some

FOURTEEN

sort, but happily it was not as serious as we first feared, and I expect him to return at any time this afternoon." Fate played into her hands at this point. "Ah! I fancy that is him now, returning from the station by taxi."

Georgie, having entrusted the unpacking of his luggage and the payment of the taxi fare to Foljambe, entered the garden-room a minute or so later, greeting Lucia, and stopping short when he beheld the Major.

"Good afternoon, Major."

"Ah, Pillson, old man. Good afternoon. Your good wife has just been informing me of your visit to your sisters. I trust that the accident was not serious."

"Thank you for your concern. Tarsome rather than serious. Hermy had been trying to jump over her ditch on a bicycle—"

"Ha! Most amusing!" commented Major Benjy.

"—but failed to reach the other side, and jarred her spine severely."

"She was very lucky she didn't break her neck," commented Lucia.

"Reminds me of an occasion in India, when old Freddie Warburton, our colonel, you know, bet us all in the Mess that he could jump over three chairs and land on his feet on the table between the soup tureen and the candlesticks. The silly b— the silly fool fell at the second fence and spent three months in the hospital with a broken collarbone. Cost him a small fortune in bets, too, I can tell you."

Georgie courteously waited until the end of this recital, and continued. "So there really was no need for me to stay, but Ursy insisted, and it would have been a waste, after all of Foljambe's hard work in packing, to have come back immediately. It is nice to be home again, though." He stopped, suddenly aware that this very house and room had been home to the Major, if only for a relatively brief time, but this fact did not seem to have registered.

"And very glad I am to have you at home again, my dear," Lucia told him.

Major Benjy still had part of his errand to fulfil – that is, ascertaining the identity of the mysterious handsome stranger who had been observed visiting Mallards. But just as Fate had just played into Lucia's hands, she now played into his.

"And where is Paolo?" asked Georgie.

"With Irene," Lucia replied. "She is working on his portrait. He will be back later this afternoon. It is so nice to see him again – he is so

FOURTEEN

different from how he was when we were on the trawler together."

Storing away the name and the information concerning the unknown visitor, and the fact that Miss Milliner Michael-Angelo, as the Major privately, and occasionally publicly, referred to Georgie, knew about the visitor, and appeared to have no objection to his existence, the Major took his leave, and sauntered down the road towards Irene in Taormina.

Fifteen

Major Benjy stood in front of Irene's door, remembering the last time he had done so. On that occasion he had walked away sadly, in a state of shock regarding the fee that Irene had demanded for what he had regarded as an easy half-day's work.

He knocked, and the bell was answered by Irene's giantess of a maid, Lucy, who looked down on him with what appeared to be a measure of disfavour.

"Miss Irene's painting at the moment, sir," she told him. "If you don't mind waiting, I'll go and see if she wants to talk to you."

She returned a minute or two later. "She'll talk to you, sir, but I've got to warn you there's a

Fifteen

model in there, so if you sit behind the screen, and only speak when she speaks to you, there'll be no problem."

Really, he thought to himself as he followed Lucy to the small conservatory that served Irene as a studio, it was worse than royalty. As he was led through the studio to the screen behind which we was to sit, he could not help but notice that a man, seemingly completely without garments, was standing in the middle of the room, and Irene, in one of the corners, was busy at the canvas.

"Now if you'll just sit there, sir, and wait until she speaks to you," Lucy told him, clearing a mass of male attire from a chair and taking them away. The Major took it that these clothes belonged to the man whose naked likeness was now being limned by Irene.

As bidden, he sat and waited for Irene to speak to him. It was not long before her voice came over.

"So, old Benjy-Wenjy, you've come to see me about Mapp's portrait, have you?"

His reaction was one of surprise mixed with relief. Naturally he was surprised that Irene had guessed the nature of his mission so accurately and quickly, and the relief sprang from

98 – Mapp's Return

the realisation that he would not have to explain his mission to her.

"How did you guess?"

"Elementary, my dear Benjy-wenjy," came the speedy answer. "It was clear that Georgie's painting of you, excellent though it is, wasn't what Mapp was expecting as a present from you. And I don't think Mapp would want anything less than a genuine Coles hanging on her wall, would she? I must say, it's taken you enough time to come here. But never mind, you're here now. So I suppose we'd better get down to the nasty subject of money."

Once more, Major Benjy was astonished by Irene's perspicacity. "Yes, if it's not a bad time to discuss the matter."

"Any time is a good time to talk about money that is going to come to me. Left shoulder a little higher. Like this. Down a little. Good, that's better. Now just stay still for another five minutes while I finish that pose."

Major Benjy guessed that these last comments were not directed at him, and waited till he was addressed directly once more. There was a long silence, and then he heard Irene's voice again.

"That's it for today, Paolo. You can put on

your clothes. Major Benjy, you can stop hiding behind that screen now."

He stood up from the chair as Lucy, who must have been listening to this conversation, appeared bearing the pile of male attire she had previously removed from the chair, and, to his great embarrassment, nearly collided with the naked youth who was returning to his garments.

"Oh never mind him," Irene called to the Major. "Though he is rather splendid, isn't he? Come and see him as the Spirit of the Age." She beckoned to her visitor and pointed to her canvas, where her model was depicted, disturbingly and flagrantly unclothed, leaning against an incongruous backdrop of shining aeroplanes, gleaming motor-cars, steam locomotives, and other mechanical marvels. "I know that Futurism is a little *passé*," she told the bemused Benjy, "but when I first saw him at Lucia's, the whole picture came into my mind all together." She stepped back, put her hands on her hips, and cocked her head to one side as she regarded the picture. "Not bad, though I say it myself. What do you think?"

Poor Major Benjy was completely taken aback. No connoisseur of art at the best of times, he was completely tongue-tied by the subject and the painting itself.

"Never mind," Irene told him. "As long as you don't tell me it's immoral or disgusting or some such rubbish, I'll just assume that you like it. Now, money. When it was going to be your portrait that you wanted me to paint, I told you seventy-five guineas, didn't I?"

He found his voice. "Yes, you did." He paused, embarrassed. "If I am to be honest with you. That is much more money than I can afford right now."

"I see," she replied. "Well, we will have to come to some sort of arrangement, won't we?"

"What sort of arrangement do you mean?" he asked, stroking his moustache nervously, more than a little conscious that he was being out-manoeuvred.

"Don't worry, I'm not going to ask you to take your clothes off." She laughed. "All I meant was that you will have to pay me a little something at the beginning, and then a little every month until the whole amount of seventy-five guineas is paid."

He heaved a sigh of relief. This was a lot less frightening than he had feared.

"But," Irene warned him, "if you don't keep

FIFTEEN

to this arrangement, the whole of Tilling will know about it."

Major Benjy shuddered inwardly. He had no doubt in his mind that Irene, quaint as she might be, was perfectly capable of carrying out her threat. He still had memories of the time when Miss Elizabeth Mapp, as she was at that time, was missing, presumed deceased, and in the expectation of her will being proved, he had treated himself to various expensive purchases made on credit. The unexpected and not wholly welcome return of the woman to whom he was now married had caused him acute embarrassment and social ignominy.

"I agree," he said.

"Then we'll say twenty-five guineas now," said Irene, "and ten every month for the next five months. How does that sound?"

He did a few quick mental calculations, and nodded. "I can manage that," he told her. "And I will tell Liz that she can expect you to visit her to paint you at Grebe next week?"

"I think that will be possible. Then we'll shake on the deal," Irene told him, extending a hand. "And no welshing on the money, you understand, or it will be all over town before you know it." They shook hands. "Sorry about that," she apologised, looking at the blue streaks that now covered the palm of the Major's hand. "A little turpentine will get rid of that."

Sixteen

While all this was going on, Lucia decided to pay a visit to the Wyses and inform Mr Wyse of what she had discovered. It would then be his responsibility as to whether he informed Susan Wyse and her daughter of the new-found status of Paolo.

Accordingly, she tripped down the hill and rang the bell of the Wyses. Figgis, Mr Wyse's valet and butler, opened the door, and Lucia asked to speak to Mr Wyse.

She was received in the front drawing room.

"Good afternoon, dear lady," Algernon Wyse greeted her. "And to what do I owe the inestimable honour of your visit here?"

"It concerns the Italian boy, Paolo Alberghi," Lucia told him.

Mr Wyse's face instantly assumed an expression of dismay. "My dear Mrs Pillson, I must apologise most profusely for my presumption in imposing such an unwelcome guest on you. I will make arrangements instantly for him to leave your house."

"You misunderstand me, I fear," Lucia told him. "I believe that you were informed that Signor Alberghi was a fisherman, and indeed, on that occasion when I and Mrs Mapp-Flint, or Miss Mapp as she was at that time, were swept out to sea in that great flood, he happened to form one of the crew of the cod trawler which plucked us from the waters."

"I understand," said Mr Wyse. "His presence reminds of you of a most disturbing and upsetting event in your past. I will make arrangements for him to leave the house for ever."

"No, you have mistaken my meaning," Lucia told him. "Paolo was one of the most kind and welcoming of all the crew of the *Allodola* – the trawler that rescued us. It is a positive pleasure to make his acquaintance once more. However, there is something about him of which possibly your Isabel has neglected to inform you – why, I do not know. It is that Paolo's father,

Sixteen

Pietro Alberghi, is apparently a rich man, and the owner of not one boat such as the *Allodola*, but at least twenty, and a factory that takes the fish caught by these boats, and prepares them for sale throughout Italy under the name *Pesce Marino Neapolitan*, according to Paolo."

Mr Wyse appeared as surprised by this information as Lucia had ever seen him. "Indeed? But why did Isabel not inform us of this? We may take it that he is telling the truth in this?"

"I see no reason to doubt it," Lucia replied.

"If true, then many of Susan and my objections to Isabel's joining herself to him will disappear. We had, I fear, marked him down as what is vulgarly known by some as a 'fortune hunter' and for that reason, though we were powerless to prevent his coming to England with Isabel, we had forbidden her to contact him while he was here."

"I confess I was wondering why she had not visited him," Lucia answered. "However, there is a slight complication." She told him of Irene's visit to Mallards. "She decided that he would make an excellent model for one of her paintings," she went on. "And I fear, from what Paolo has told me, that he was at least partially unclothed as he sat for her."

"Dear me," said Mr Wyse. "I am somewhat

shocked at the news. Miss Coles undoubtedly possesses artistic talent of a very high order, but she may, in her occasional attitude to conventional morals, be described as..."

"Quaint." Lucia finished the sentence for him.

Mr Wyse bowed. "An excellent epithet," he said. "But do you consider that this has had any kind of damaging effect on the lad?"

"I fear so. He has – temporarily, let us hope, transferred the object of his adoration from Isabel, for whom he had previously expressed the highest regard, to Irene Coles. He will, I am certain, receive no response from her – I believe that Dr Freud has written something regarding such unpleasant matters – and it is of course quite possible, or even likely, that his affections will return to your step-daughter. I will endeavour to persuade him of his error, and encourage this – of course only should you approve of this course of action."

"I see," Mr Wyse mused. "A most embarrassing position for all concerned, Miss Coles included. Given what the lad has told us of his family's circumstances, I at least have few worries regarding any possible attachment he may form with regard to Isabel, and I am certain that Susan will be of the same mind."

"However, it may be as well to confirm this,"

Sixteen

Lucia said to him. "It occurs to me that your sister Amelia, the Contessa, would be able to make enquiries in Italy and confirm or deny the story. Perhaps you might telegraph and ascertain what knowledge she might have, or discover, to confirm what I have been told?"

"An excellent idea. I will send a telegram instantly. Since Isabel did not see fit to inform her mother or me of this Paolo's origins, it is quite likely, however, that she also failed to impart the information to Amelia and Cecco." Mr Wyse paused. "In the meantime," he went on, "What would you propose that we do with regard to this matter?"

"I feel Irene's embarrassment should be the least of our worries. She is, after all, a most independent character. It may be that we need to do nothing on that score – after all, she will not wish to paint his picture for ever, and that he will then find her door closed to him. She certainly possesses enough strength of character to clarify her feelings on the matter to him. At that point, should you believe him to be an acceptable suitor, I feel that it might prove judicious to invite him here to meet Isabel, or for her to visit him at Mallards."

"I will have to consult Susan about this, of course, but your proposal seems like a good one to me. Believe me, dear lady, I am more than grateful to you for your generosity and forbearance, not to mention the considerable trouble that you have taken to apprise me of this delicate matter."

"Believe me, it is a genuine pleasure for my husband and me to have him as a guest. Other than his romantic entanglements, and much may be excused on that score, I feel, on account of his youth, he has been a perfect guest."

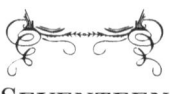

SEVENTEEN

Major Benjamin Mapp-Flint was delighted that he had been able to fulfil all his errands. He had been able to name the mysterious visitor to Mallards as Paolo and discovered something of his origins; he had seen the visitor with his own eyes (though indeed he had seen more of him that was needed or desired); and he had negotiated an arrangement with Irene, albeit long overdue, with regard to a birthday gift to his wife which would, he hoped, bring about something in the nature of a lasting peace.

With that in mind, he took himself to the country club of which he was a member, and demanded a whisky and soda. The barman,

Seventeen

who was well aware of Major Benjy's tastes, and who was also well aware of the fact that the police constable who might otherwise raise any objection was safely in bed with measles on the other side of Tilling, served him despite the hour of the day. One whisky and soda led to another, and yet another, so that by the time came for Major Benjy to return to Grebe, he was well-primed for the journey.

It took him a little longer than he had anticipated to arrive back at the house, due to the road's unfortunate habit of suddenly appearing to change direction as he walked along it, but he eventually reached Grebe, in a slightly more composed state than when he had started his journey. However, it would have been an error to describe him as being sober.

"All sorted out now, Liz," he announced proudly. "Here's your book from Lucia. Told her you had a sprained ankle. Useful thing to have, what? It can get better whenever you want it to, eh?" He laughed. Although the Dante had somehow managed to escape his grasp a few times on the journey home, he still had it with him, a fact that amazed him when he came to consider it.

She received it with a chilly word of thanks, well aware from the sound and smell of his

Seventeen

laughter that whisky had played a part in his doings of the afternoon.

"And I arranged for your picture to be painted," he told her. "Irene Coles will come here next week."

"And else what did you find out?" she asked him. "What about Lucia's visitor?"

"His name's Paolo. Some sort of foreigner, probably Italian. She mentioned something about him being on the trawler that time of the flood when you were both on the table."

Elizabeth pursed her lips and furrowed her brow in concentration. "Yes, I do remember there was one of the crew called Paolo. A youngish lad, and some might call him quite good-looking in a foreign sort of way, if their tastes ran to that sort of thing, that is. Lucia spent a lot of time with him, I remember, pretending to learn how to tie knots and that sort of thing. Her fingers intertwined with his as they laughed and chattered away. It must be the same lad." She sighed heavily. "I wonder how she managed to discover him to invite him over from Italy to stay with her. And what will Mr Georgie have to say about this, I wonder?"

"Oh, he returned while I was there."

"Where had he been?"

The Major was forced to think for a while

before he remembered the details. "Most amusing. One of his sisters—"

"I don't think we have ever met them, have we?" Elizabeth asked suspiciously. "Do they really exist, I wonder?"

Her husband continued. "One of his sisters had tried to jump over a ditch while riding a bicycle, it seems, and had injured herself."

"I cannot say I am surprised," Elizabeth commented.

"And so Miss Milliner Michael-Angelo went to be with her, but it turned out not to be as serious as they had believed at first, and so he came back."

"What did he have to say about this Paolo?"

"Not a lot. Asked where he was." Major Benjy yawned. The combination of the fresh air on his walk back to Grebe, combined with the whisky, had suddenly made him feel very tired.

"And you saw this Italian sailor?"

"Ha! Did I see him?" Major Benjy laughed immoderately. "I saw all of him!"

"What do you mean?" asked his wife.

"He was not wearing any clothes at all, not a stitch."

"What?" she exclaimed. "What was going on?"

"She was painting his picture."

Seventeen

"Good heavens!" Elizabeth was genuinely shocked. "I would never have imagined..." She drew a tactful veil over whatever it was that she had never imagined. Even so, lurid thoughts kept making their way into her mind. "And she invited you in while this was going on?"

"Yes. Though she did ask me to sit behind a screen while she was painting." He yawned again.

"Poor boy," Elizabeth said. "Why don't you go and have a little nap before dinner?" Her voice was calm, but inwardly she was exulting.

She had always known Lucia to be not quite 'the thing', or if she had not known it, she had always been seeking the evidence that would allow her to say that she had always known it. For she had taken Major Benjy's story of nude models, and the attendant depravity and loose living, to refer to Lucia, while he, assuming that she would automatically realise that he was referring to Irene, had omitted to assign a name to the artist.

Elizabeth's mind seethed. She had voiced her belief as to Lucia's morals — or at least hinted at her suspicions by denying them to Diva — on their return from the Gallagher Banks. Then there was Georgie's behaviour, visiting the undeniably glamorous Olga Braceley in

France, and, if rumour was true, flirting with Duchesses, no less. On the one hand, any behaviour such as Lucia's was to be strongly censured. But on the other hand…

In a flash, Elizabeth's plan of action became dazzlingly clear. Lucia should not be the only woman in Tilling with a handsome young lover, for by now in Elizabeth's mind Paolo had been promoted to this status as far as Lucia was concerned. As to who should play the role of this lover, it was clear that it was in Elizabeth's interest – indeed, it was her moral duty to save Lucia from her own nature – to detach this Paolo from Lucia and claim him for herself as an admirer, devoted to her and her alone.

As her admirer, she would be able to rebuff him, gently but decisively, and retain a moral high ground from which she could look down and castigate Lucia without exposing herself to the charge of hypocrisy. As far as the details were concerned, she could, after all, claim prior acquaintance through their time on the trawler together, and she could now remember clearly the many occasions at that time when he had smiled on her, or talked affectionately to her – or if she could not exactly remember them, she had as clear a picture in her mind of these events as if they had actually occurred.

Seventeen

It would be a simple matter, she told herself, for her to point out the obvious disadvantages of the more elderly, if only by a few years, Lucia, when compared to the younger and clearly more attractive Elizabeth Mapp. For she determined, when renewing her acquaintance with Paolo, to un-Flint herself, and to make no mention of Major Benjy if it could be at all avoided.

Withers entered the room to announce dinner, and Elizabeth went into the dining-room to attack the beef cutlets with a renewed appetite.

Eighteen

The next day saw Elizabeth in Tilling, her marketing basket on her arm, hobbling artistically from shop to shop, changing the afflicted ankle between left and right when out of sight of others. As she passed the shop of Hopkins, the fishmonger's, she was reminded of the time some years ago when she had visited Irene and discovered the man from whom she regularly ordered her sole and plaice clad only in a pair of small bathing-drawers. But then Irene Coles was a recognised artist, and Hopkins had been decently, if skimpily, clad. While in this case...

She was working herself into a state of

EIGHTEEN

righteous indignation when Diva appeared around the corner, moving, as always, at high speed.

"Any news?" Elizabeth asked.

"Seventeen shilling teas and five eighteen-penny ones yesterday. Tried a new recipe for sardine tartlets yesterday. Dash of cayenne pepper. People like it."

"No, I meant any news about Lucia's young man."

"Oh, Mr Georgie? Saw him this morning, back from wherever he has been. Didn't speak with him."

"He went to visit his sisters, at least that's what I've been told," Elizabeth said, in a tone that clearly indicated that she doubted the veracity of whoever had given her that information. "One of these sisters had some sort of an accident which needed his attention."

"But he's back now," Diva objected.

"So he is," Elizabeth agreed, in what she imagined to be a meaningful voice. "But I wasn't talking about Mr Georgie. Hardly what one would describe as 'young' any more, is he, with his hair and everything. I was referring to Lucia's young man whose acquaintance she first made on the Italian trawler. The one with whom she was – and apparently still is – so, shall we say, friendly."

"You mean—?"

"I only know what I have been told, and I am not at all sure that it is proper to repeat it. Jezebel's not in it."

"Then you'd better not repeat it if it's not proper," Diva said decisively.

"Very well," Elizabeth answered crossly, annoyed at not being pressed to provide the details.

The two ladies bade each other a frosty farewell, and Elizabeth, still vexed at not having provided the story of the nude model, was nevertheless pleased that she had at least managed to sow the seeds of suspicion on ground that she sincerely hoped would not prove to be stony, but would bear fruit as Diva circulated around the town.

On turning the next corner, she came into contact with the Padre and Evie Bartlett.

"What ho! A good morrow to ye, fair dame," he cried. "What a bonny day it is, in troth. And is there any news to be had this morn?"

Elizabeth considered that she had to be a little less direct with the Padre than she had been with Elizabeth. "Lucia and Georgie..." she began.

Eighteen

"Hoots awa', woman," replied the Padre. "We met with Maister Georgie anon, and the puir wee mannie was telling us about his sisters."

"They live in Wiltshire," squeaked Evie, emerging from the shadow of her husband. "He told us that they had had some sort of accident with a bicycle, and that one of them had broken her back, they thought, so he went to see them."

"And Lucia's visitor...?" Elizabeth probed gently. "Her young man?"

"Och, I ken nothing about any visitor, young or old." replied the Padre.

"The rather good-looking young Italian who has been staying at Mallards while Mr Georgie was away with whoever it was."

"Whatever do you mean?" asked Evie.

"I should say no more. You know how I hate repeating gossipy rumours," Elizabeth told her. This was, to a large extent, true. She much preferred starting such undercurrents of conversation, rather than merely repeating them.

"Why? Whatever do you mean by that?" Evie repeated.

Elizabeth said nothing, but her eloquent silence, combined with what she fondly believed to be a Sphinx-like enigmatic smile, did more than mere words could ever have achieved in arousing curiosity in the breasts of her hearers.

She wondered whether to visit Irene with her news, but on reflection decided against it. If Irene was coming to paint her portrait, any offence caused by references to Lucia, whom Elizabeth was well aware was held in high regard by Irene, might well manifest itself in unflattering quaint touches in her painted likeness.

However, there were still the Wyses, in whose collective path heavy hints, though of the most tactful nature, remained to be dropped. Some judicious loitering was required, but Elizabeth's patience was eventually rewarded by the sight of Susan's great Royce making its way along the High Street, with a mass of sables in the back seat and what appeared to be a spiky-haired ragamuffin sitting beside her.

As the great car drew alongside Elizabeth, it stopped, and the window opened. "Elizabeth dear, you remember Isabel, do you not?" asked the heap of sables, motioning to the ragamuffin.

"Ah, dear Isabel," cooed Elizabeth. "How well you look. Where have you been?"

"Oh, here and there," was the reply.

"Isabel and I were wondering, were we not, Isabel, if you would care to join us for tea this

Eighteen

afternoon at three o'clock. Of course, I will send the Royce to Grebe to collect you and arrange for you to be returned in the same way, if that would be convenient. Do say yes – just the three of us."

It was unusual for Susan to extend such an invitation at such short notice – indeed, a tea-party for three was somewhat unusual in itself, and Elizabeth, intuiting that there was some ulterior motive behind the invitation, and anxious to discover exactly what it was that lay behind that particular curtain, accepted both the Royce and the tea.

"Sweet of you to offer, dear Susan," she smiled. "Delightful. I accept your kind offer with the greatest of pleasure."

With that, the Royce moved on, and Elizabeth was left to contemplate with pleasure the words that she would use to hint at Lucia's brazen immorality. As if to complete her plans, she recognised the young Italian fisherman making his way down the street in her direction. There was no time like the present, she said to herself, to start her platonic seduction of Paolo.

Her sprained ankle became visibly more painful as she moved towards him, eyes downcast so that she might collide with him as a result of pure chance. When this event occurred, she raised her eyes, and allowed a look for surprised recognition to spread over her face.

"Why, I know you!" she exclaimed, her great smile showing her pleasure at the recognition. "You were on the fishing boat that rescued me and Lucia from the sea on that dreadful day."

"Sí, sí, yes, yes." His smiling face showed that the recognition was mutual. "You are the other one. The one who was so sick many times."

This was something of which Elizabeth did not care to be reminded, nor was she enthralled by his characterisation of her as 'the other one'. Never mind, she said to herself. There was plenty of time to bring Paolo round to the correct way of thinking.

"And why are you in Tilling?" she said slowly and carefully, unsure of his understanding of English.

"Ah, I am in love," he said. "This town has so many beautiful ladies, but there is one special for me."

It was not Elizabeth's way to force a frontal assault on the truth. She preferred flanking methods, which would achieve the same end, but by a more circuitous route.

"And where are you staying? At the Trader's Arms?"

Eighteen

"No, no. I am staying in the arms of Lucia." He pointed towards Mallards.

"That's nice," said Elizabeth. How, she demanded of herself, was she to wrest him from Lucia's arms and, metaphorically at least, into her own? She took a step forward and staggered a little as her ankle seemed to give way.

"Oh, you are hurt," Paolo told her. "*Povera signora.* Where do you go? I help you."

"Oh, it is so far," she told him.

"*Non è niente.* It is nothing," he said, and before she had fully realised what was happening, he had seized her marketing basket which, truth to tell, was not very cumbersome, and she found herself leaning heavily on him, as he supported her arm on the side of her supposed bad ankle.

She had her doubts as to whether she would be able to maintain the painful ankle all the way to Grebe, but in the meantime, she was clinging in a most intimate and yet decorous fashion to a handsome young Italian – Lucia's handsome young Italian at that – in full view of all Tilling.

Nineteen

While the above conversation was taking place, Diva and the Bartletts had met outside Twemlow's, the grocer's. The topic of conversation was, hardly surprisingly, the news that Elizabeth Mapp-Flint had delicately failed to convey to them. In his excitement, the Padre had forgotten to be either Scotch or medieval.

"But what exactly was it that she was hinting at?" he asked.

"A young man. Met him on the Italian trawler that time she and Lucia were washed out to sea," said Diva.

The Padre frowned. "I fail to understand.

Nineteen

What relevance to today has an acquaintance made several years ago under such circumstances?"

"Elizabeth referred to him as Lucia's young man," said Diva. "And with my own eyes I saw him in the garden-room talking with Lucia." This was a slight exaggeration. Diva seen only part of a trouser-leg of the unidentified visitor through the garden-room window, and had only later seen a young man who might or might not have been this mysterious Italian fisherman apparently admitted to Mallards, and who might or might not have been the wearer of the anonymous trousers seen through the window. These inferences were perhaps justified when disseminating Tilling news, but would not have passed muster in a police-court. "And," Diva added in conspiratorial tones, "she mentioned Jezebel."

"Not about Lucia, surely," said Evie. "I mean, she is not perfect, but..." She stopped short of enumerating the areas in which Lucia might or might not fall short of perfection.

"We must not judge," said the Padre, in judgemental tones. "Whatever faults a poor sinner may have, it is not for us to condemn them."

Neither lady felt able to answer this, and the

meeting broke up as the parties went their different ways.

Diva's next meeting was with Georgie, who was standing outside the haberdasher's, comparing silks.

"Good morning, Mrs Plaistow," he said, raising his hat to her. "If you have a minute or two, I would welcome your advice. It concerns Lucia, but I don't want her to know about it."

Diva, hoping and fearing that she would be drawn into some confidential secret connected with what Elizabeth had so eloquently failed to state, agreed.

"I'm embroidering a petit point cushion cover for her birthday. It will be a picture of her secret garden, the design for which I sketched myself. The trouble is that I am not sure what colour of silk I should be using for the leaves of the fig tree. Is this green too light, do you think? Or this one? I really cannot decide. Most tarsome."

Diva, disappointed that the secret was of such a trivial variety and did not concern anything of a nature that might possibly be considered immoral, chose one of the threads without overly concerning herself as to whether it matched the fig-tree or not.

Nineteen

"So kind of you," said Georgie. "That's what I was thinking, too. Thank you."

Diva decided to take the bull by the horns. "Someone mentioned that you have a guest staying at Mallards." She waited expectantly, wondering whether she might not have gone a little too far.

However, she need not have worried. Georgie smiled. "Yes, we have a young Italian man staying with us. Quite a coincidence, really. He was on that Italian fishing boat that picked up Lucia and Elizabeth in that time of the great flood. It gave Lucia quite a surprise when they recognised each other. Charming boy, though. It has been a real pleasure to have Paolo as a guest." He remembered one of the supposed benefits of Paolo's visit. "And it is such a pleasure for us to be able to speak Italian with him."

Diva was puzzled about the coincidental nature of the guest's identity. "When you invited him, were you not aware that he had been on that boat?"

"Ah, but you see..." Georgie's voice grew low and conspiratorial. "The invitation to stay at Mallards did not come from Lucia or me."

"From whom, then?" asked Diva, by now thoroughly intrigued.

"I am afraid I cannot say more at the moment,"

Georgie told her. His tone was polite, but firm. "I am sure that the details will be made public soon."

Diva's level of interest, already at what she had imagined to be its peak, now soared to impossible heights, but she bit her tongue to prevent her asking a multitude of questions, and merely nodded silently.

As Georgie left her, and made his way back to Mallards, Diva glimpsed an unusual couple who had just come into view at the other end of the street. Elizabeth, still noticeably limping (though Diva was fairly sure that the affected leg had changed from when she had spoken with her), was leaning heavily on the arm of a young man who was carrying her marketing basket.

As speedily and as stealthily as she could, Diva hurried up the street to catch a glimpse of the mysterious stranger who had attached himself to Elizabeth. His features came into clearer focus, and to her astonishment, Diva beheld someone who could be none other than Lucia's Italian visitor.

Thoughts raced through Diva's active imagination. Were Elizabeth's delicate evasions actually diversions, designed to deflect attention from her own dalliance with this Italian,

NINETEEN

with whom it was clear that she already had an acquaintance? Diva hardly believed that this could be so, especially since this Paolo was staying at Mallards. And yet... there was the evidence of her own eyes.

In a kind of dream, Diva made her way back to Wasters, determined to get to the bottom of this mystery before too long.

Twenty

Happily, Major Benjy was not at home when Elizabeth, still supported by Paolo, arrived at Grebe. Although she had initially wanted her supposed attachment to the handsome young Italian to be noticed by the inhabitants of Tilling, Elizabeth was unsure as to how this might be received by her husband, especially since he had apparently last seen the lad in a state of undress.

"Thank you, Paolo. *Grazie*," she thanked him, summoning up one of her few words of Italian. She offered an invitation to stay for lunch in such a manner that she felt sure he would not accept, and to her relief, he declined, saying

TWENTY

that he was expected at Lucia's, and started to make his way back to Tilling.

All through lunch, which was eaten together with Major Benjy, Elizabeth sat silently plotting the next step in her plan of campaign, which would be executed at the tea with Susan and Isabel later that afternoon. Though she had chosen the most circuitous route from the centre of Tilling to Grebe in order to be seen with Paolo, she was still unsure as to how widely she had been observed, or how far the news might have spread.

At the appointed time, the Royce swept up to the front gate of Grebe, and Elizabeth, with the artful use of a stick, entered the vehicle and was carried off to the Wyse residence.

"Dear Susan, how good of you to invite this poor invalid," she greeted her hostess. "And sweet Isabel, how well you are looking."

"Isabel has been staying in Capri with my sister-in-law, Amelia, Contessa Faraglione and her husband, the Count – Cecco, you know."

Bells started to chime in Elizabeth's mind. She well remembered Amelia and her visits to Tilling – indeed, it would be a long time before she forgot that disastrous occasion in this very house when she was convinced that she had at last exposed Lucia's claims to fluency in the Italian language. Instead, Lucia had by means unknown established herself as having a perfect mastery in written Italian (though it still seemed strange to Elizabeth that neither Lucia nor Georgie were aware of the Italian word for paperknife).

But she well remembered that the island of Capri was close to Naples, and that the *Allodola*, the fishing boat which had plucked her and Lucia from the frigid waters of the English Channel, had originated from that city, and that Paolo had been a member of the *Allodola*'s crew. Was it perhaps possible that...?

"How delightful," she said to Isabel. "I am sure that you were made to feel most welcome there."

As far as Elizabeth was able to ascertain, Isabel appeared to blush under her heavy sunburn as she stammered a reply in the affirmative.

No one who knew Elizabeth Mapp-Flint at all could accuse her of being unwilling to put two and two together. The fact that she arrived at three or five as the solution as often as she arrived at four was of little consequence in her eyes.

On this occasion, she assembled the facts

TWENTY

known to her and unerringly arrived at the wrong answer. "And that charming young man of Lucia's – Paolo, is it not? – hails from that area, I believe."

The effect of this speech was shattering. Isabel turned pale under her tan, and positively ran out of the room. The sound of sobbing could be heard from the next room.

Susan Wyse turned to Elizabeth with a look of reproach mixed with what might have passed for anger in one a little more forceful, but said nothing. It was clearly incumbent upon Elizabeth to mend whatever fences she had carelessly broken.

"I beg your pardon," she said. "I had no intention of upsetting dear Isabel just then."

The ball was now obviously in Susan's court, and it was up to her to provide an explanation of the recent catastrophe, but no such elucidation appeared to be forthcoming.

Tepid tea was sipped, and scones nibbled in near-silence, broken only by noncommittal remarks regarding the weather, and the price of dabs in Hopkins, the fishmonger's.

Once these topics of conversation had been exhausted, Elizabeth felt it was incumbent upon her to go.

"Poor Benjy-boy," she said, with a sad little

moue. "Not quite the thing this morning. I really should go home to look after him."

For her part, Susan made a protestation at the thought of Elizabeth's departure, but as she ordered Figgis to arrange the Royce for Elizabeth's convenience while she was doing so, it might justifiably have been assumed that she was somewhat less than sincere in her regret at her guest's leaving.

Twenty-One

On the following morning, Diva Plaistow, having completed both the filling of her marketing basket with ingredients for her round of afternoon teas, and (only slightly less tempting) her mind with the ingredients for a good round of gossip, met Evie and the Padre in the High Street.

"Such news," she said breathlessly before either Bartlett was able to speak. "But not here. Come with me." Beckoning to the bemused couple to follow, she led the way to her house, where she invited her guests to sit at one of the tea-tables that would be used by her customers that afternoon.

The three, almost instinctively, leaned over

the table, craning their necks as if not to allow any word passing between them to escape. The overall picture was similar to the Three Witches hunched over a cauldron at the start of *Macbeth*, and the resemblance was enhanced when Janet, following Diva's request as she entered the house, brought in a steaming teapot and three cups.

As she poured the tea, Diva spoke. "It's Elizabeth. Again."

"Why, what mischief has the lassie been up to the noo?" asked the Padre.

"Better ask what she has not been doing," Diva said darkly. "That Italian lad staying at Mallards."

"Aye?"

"I saw Elizabeth walking arm in arm with him yesterday." She paused, confident that her audience would demand more from her. She was not disappointed. "And," she went on, "only this morning I saw her go to Mallards and drop an envelope through the letter-box. Five minutes later, out came this Paolo. And he kissed her on both cheeks!"

"No!" squeaked Evie.

"Oh yes indeed. And then, without as much as a by your leave, he took her basket from her, and put his arm through hers, cool and calm

Twenty-One

as you like, and off they strolled together. So what do you think of that?" she concluded triumphantly.

"I dinna ken what we should be thinking," said the Padre. "There was Mistress Mapp, trying to make us all believe that there wee mannie was— well, best not be saying what she was hinting to us."

"And all the time," Evie burst in, "she was—"

Diva leaned forward even more conspiratorially, if that were possible. "I haven't told you the half of it," she said. The other two members of the coven also drew closer so that their heads were almost touching. "I talked to Mr Georgie yesterday," Diva told them in a hoarse half-whisper. "He told me that this Paolo was not invited to Mallards by him or by Lucia, and that he – I mean Paolo, of course – had been one of the crew on that fishing boat that rescued Lucia and one other person from the kitchen table. And," she concluded triumphantly, "we know who that other person is, don't we?"

A look of shock spread over Evie's face as she absorbed this information. "And Elizabeth was telling us— well, not really telling us, but hinting — that Lucia and this Paolo were…" She tailed off, leaving the others to imagine for

138 – *Mapp's Return*

themselves about the subject of Elizabeth's hints.

"I really feel I should have a word with her about this," said the Padre, slipping south of the border into the present day.

"Hah!" Diva said to him. "You'd get four or five words back for every one you gave to her. And I know what kind of words they would be."

"Even so," said the Padre. "There is more rejoicing over one sheep that was lost…" but he failed to pursue the image, as it strained even his powers of belief to picture Elizabeth as a misplaced woolly ruminant.

"Dear me," mused Evie. "What times we live in." There was little more to be said, and the trio finished their tea before making their separate ways; the Bartletts to the Vicarage, and Diva deep in thought as she started to mix the dough for the afternoon's scones.

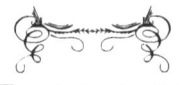

Twenty-two

A few days later, Elizabeth Mapp-Flint was still somewhat perplexed as to the nature of the crime she had committed at Susan Wyse's. That it had been a misdemeanour of great seriousness was obvious, and she had been cut by Susan three times since then as they came close to each other on the street, and on one of those occasions Isabel, who had been accompanying her mother, literally turned and fled from the sight of Elizabeth.

In addition to this, it was noticeable that Diva Plaistow, whenever she beheld Elizabeth at the other end of the street, immediately turned her back, and hurried away in the opposite direction. Rack her brains as she would, she was unable to recall any personal insult directed towards Diva, still less towards the Padre and Evie, who seemed determined to follow Diva's lead in the matter.

At the same time, Major Benjy, whose perceptions of the finer feelings were not always of the finest, discovered what appeared to be a more sympathetic manner in his dealings with the Padre. Twice in their latest game of golf, the Padre had generously allowed a mulligan in conditions where the Major would have definitely denied one, and had furthermore generously paid for the drinks in the bar afterwards. At several points during the game, he had appeared to be about to speak with an expression of great seriousness visible on his face, but on each occasion he had suddenly drawn back, as if his nerve had somehow failed him.

She returned from her marketing in a bad mood. She had planned another bridge afternoon for later in the week, but with the Wyses obviously out of the picture as potential invitees, and Diva and the Bartletts seemingly determined to cut her, that left only Lucia and Georgie as potential bridge players, and that was clearly out of the question.

After lunch, Benjy went off to his golf, and she sat in a chair considering her next move.

TWENTY-TWO

Her brooding was interrupted by a knock on the door, and a rather disapproving Withers announced the arrival of Irene Coles.

"Hello, Mapp, old girl," Irene greeted her. "Dear old Major Benjy has commissioned me to paint you in the most flattering of lights, and so here I am, ready to do battle with truth in his service. Quai hai, what?"

"You mean, you want to paint me this afternoon?"

"Yes, I intend to start this afternoon, unless you would prefer me to go away and paint something else."

"But I'm not wearing the clothes that I want to be painted in."

"Doesn't matter. I'm only going to do the preliminary sketches today. We can choose the clothes later. Or perhaps you would prefer to be painted without clothes. That's always a possibility, of course."

"Certainly not!"

"Keep your hair on, Mapp. I was only joking. Of course, there are some who prefer to be painted without their clothes on. That young Paolo, for example."

"Oh, you heard about that, did you?"

"I didn't just hear about it, I made it happen. My next masterpiece going to the Academy will be Paolo, posed as the Spirit of the Age. And a jolly fine Spirit of the Age he is, too."

"So it was you who was painting him with no clothes on?"

"Of course. Who else among you Philistines of Tilling is unafraid of naked flesh?"

Elizabeth was confused. "I had thought that perhaps Lucia..."

Irene threw back her head and laughed raucously. "Oh, my dear Mapp. Lucia painting a nude model? What an imagination you must have, to be sure. Can you really see Lucia doing that?"

Now that Elizabeth came to think about it, it seemed extremely unlikely that Lucia would ever be capable of such a thing. "But, but... Major Benjy told me that he had seen this Paolo with no clothes on."

"That's right," Irene agreed brightly. "When he came to ask me about this picture I'm about to do of you, I was busy painting Paolo."

"But he said..." Her voice trailed off as she struggled to recall exactly what her husband had said to her. As far as she could remember he had been somewhat under the influence of drink when he had told her about Paolo's nude modelling. Could he have made such an error.

Twenty-Two

Worse, could she herself really have made such a dreadful mistake?

"But Paolo is in love with Lucia, isn't he?" Surely this was no figment of her imagination.

Again, Irene's laugh filled the room. "Now where on earth did you get that idea from?"

"He told me so himself." But once more, doubts filled her mind. Had she been only too ready to believe what she wanted to be true, and twisted Paolo's words to fit her own imaginings?

"Let me tell you the whole story, sweet one," Irene cooed. "Dear Lucia has been telling me all about it." Elizabeth ignored the cruel parody of her own tones, and seated herself back in her chair, prepared to listen.

"The reason Paolo is in Tilling because of Isabel Poppit, who has been staying with the Contessa Faradiddleony," Irene began. "You knew him only as a fisherman on that boat which you shared with Lucia, but Lucia tells me that Paolo says his father is a rich man who owns many boats and a factory for preserving fish, and that the tinned fish is sold all over Italy. The Wyses have asked the Contessa to enquire if Paolo's account is true, and it seems that it is. Paolo is a very wealthy young man, it seems, or at least his family is very rich, which comes to much the same thing."

Elizabeth sat entranced.

"Close your mouth, Mapp," Irene commanded. "It doesn't suit you at all to go round looking like one of Paolo's father's fishes. Anyway, this Paolo met Isabel while she was in Italy, and... well, they liked each other, as you might say. When it was time for Isabel to come back to England, she told Susan and Algernon that she was bringing Paolo with her."

"So Lucia didn't invite him to stay with her? He wasn't in love with her?" Elizabeth said, stunned by this flood of information.

"No, of course not," Irene said impatiently. "Lucia told me that Algernon had visited her and asked her to have Paolo as a guest at Mallards, since he and Susan disliked the idea of having an Italian fisherman who was in love with Isabel staying with them. Of course, no one ever dreamed that he had been on your trawler."

Elizabeth's only answer to this was a weak "Oh," as if she had been punched in the stomach.

"Algernon asked her to keep all this a secret, of course, but now the cat's out of the bag, and all can be revealed. Of course, when Paolo

TWENTY-TWO

arrived, Lucia and he were very pleased to see each other. But as for him being in love with Lucia, or Lucia being in love with him, I don't know how you ever came to believe that." Irene paused. "It is true, though, that for a day or two he transferred his affections to another." She paused, enjoying the sensations that came from teasing Elizabeth.

"Who was that, quaint one?" Elizabeth asked through gritted teeth.

"Why me, of course. Somehow he had got it into his head that a woman who asked him to take off his clothes and paint his portrait was in love with him, and the least he could do was to return her feelings. Well, I wasn't going to have any of that, now, was I? So I told him in no uncertain terms that I wouldn't put up with his nonsense, and that his place was with Isabel, and Lucia and Georgie told him the same."

"And now?"

"Paolo has been to visit Isabel at the Wyses', and they thoroughly approve of him. He's a nice boy, after all. Isabel's happy, Paolo's happy, I'm happy, and so are Lucia and Georgie. The snail's on the wing and the lark's on the thorn – or something – and all's well with the world."

Elizabeth sat numb, her mind filled with the

hideous realities that now swept through her mind.

"And another thing, Mapp," Irene went on. "Diva and Evie have been going round telling people how you were accusing Lucia of— well, never mind exactly what it was that you went around hinting. And all the time, you yourself were flirting with Paolo. Lucia tells me that Paolo told her that you fluttered your eyelashes at him. Oh, do flutter your eyelashes at me, dear one. I do so want to see what it looks like."

"Certainly not," snapped Elizabeth, by now wishing herself anywhere but where she was, but at the same time desperate to hear more.

"Well, if you won't, you won't. Anyway, Paolo is a perfect gentleman, and when he saw you hobbling along the street, he felt duty-bound to help you. Hope you're grateful. How is the ankle, by the way?"

"Much better, thank you." Elizabeth was curt.

"So I noticed," Irene observed acidly. She paused. "So, about the portrait..."

"Oh, get out!" Elizabeth screamed at her. "Get out of here! I never want to see you or any of them ever again!" Rage and humiliation boiled within her as she realised it would be months before the incidents of the past weeks would

Twenty-Two

be forgotten and forgiven. Until that time, she dared not show her face in Tilling.

The front door slammed as Irene made her way out of Grebe, and left Elizabeth sitting distraught in the empty room. Tears of frustration welled in her eyes as the sun started to set over the marsh.

If you enjoyed this story...

Please consider writing a review on a Web site such as Amazon or Goodreads.

You may also enjoy some adventures of Sherlock Holmes by Hugh Ashton, who has been described in *The District Messenger*, the newsletter of the Sherlock Holmes Society of London, as being "one of the best writers of new Sherlock Holmes stories, in both plotting and style".

Volumes published so far include :

Tales from the Deed Box of John H. Watson M.D.
More from the Deed Box of John H. Watson M.D.
Secrets from the Deed Box of John H. Watson M.D.
The Darlington Substitution (novel)
Notes from the Dispatch-Box of John H. Watson M.D.
Further Notes from the Dispatch-box of John H. Watson M.D.
The Death of Cardinal Tosca (novel)
The Last Notes from the Dispatch-box of John H. Watson, M.D.
The Trepoff Murder (ebook only)
1894
Without my Boswell

If you enjoyed this story...

Some Singular Cases of Mr. Sherlock Holmes
The Lichfield Murder
The Adventure of the Bloody Steps
The Adventure of Vanaprastha (ebook only)

Children's detective stories, with beautiful illustrations by Andy Boerger, the first of which was nominated for the prestigious Caldecott Prize :

Sherlock Ferret and the Missing Necklace
Sherlock Ferret and The Multiplying Masterpieces
Sherlock Ferret and The Poisoned Pond
Sherlock Ferret and the Phantom Photographer
The Adventures of Sherlock Ferret

Short stories, thrillers, alternative history, and historical science fiction titles:

Tales of Old Japanese
At the Sharpe End
Balance of Powers
Beneath Gray Skies
Red Wheels Turning
Angels Unawares
The Untime
The Untime Revisited
Unknown Quantities
Mapp at Fifty

Full details of all of these and more at :
https://HughAshtonBooks.com

About the Author

Hugh Ashton was born in the United Kingdom, and moved to Japan in 1988, where he lived until his return to the UK in 2016.

He is best known for his Sherlock Holmes stories, which have been hailed as some of the most authentic pastiches on the market, and have received favourable reviews from Sherlockians and non-Sherlockians alike.

He has also published other work in a number of genres, including alternative history, historical science fiction, and thrillers, based in Japan, the USA, and the UK.

He currently lives in the historic city of Lichfield with his wife, Yoshiko.

His ramblings may be found on Facebook, Twitter, and in various other places on the Internet. He may be contacted at: author@HughAshtonBooks.com

CPSIA information can be obtained
at www.ICGtesting.com
Printed in the USA
LVHW040926240222
711913LV00002B/142